SEA-WYF

Books by J. M. SCOTT

THE WILL AND THE WAY

HEATHER MARY

THE MAN WHO MADE WINE

THE OTHER HALF OF THE ORANGE

SEA-WYF

SEA-WYF

by

J. M. SCOTT

E. P. DUTTON & COMPANY, INC.

NEW YORK, 1956

LIBRARY OF CONGRESS CATALOG CARD NUMBER: 56–5257

SEA-WYF

CHAPTER ONE

On Wednesday, March 7, 1951, the following announcement appeared in the Personal Column of the London *Daily Telegraph*:

> SEA-WYF. Home at last. Please get
> in touch. BISCUIT

There was no response. On March 12 came a second appeal:

> SEA-WYF. Have returned with fatted
> calf but no unsuitable memories. Please
> get in touch. BISCUIT.

Still no reply. So, on March 16:

> SEA-WYF. Am certain you are alive.
> Are you afraid of past or me?
> BISCUIT.

Sea-Wyf remained silent. On March 21 the tone of the announcement changed:

> SEA-WYF. Intend to find you by pub-
> lishing story of fourteen weeks and
> Number Four. BISCUIT.

SEA-WYF

That did draw a response—but not from Sea-Wyf. On March 26 this announcement appeared:

> BISCUIT. The compact is still more vital after these nine years.
> BULLDOG.

Biscuit replied at once:

> BULLDOG. Thanks for confirming Sea-Wyf is alive. Please put in touch.
> BISCUIT.

Then:

> BISCUIT. Do not know Sea-Wyf's whereabouts, but we three are alive and useful. Why resurrect Noah's Ark and Number Four? BULLDOG.

Biscuit was not diverted. On April 6 he replied:

> BULLDOG. Number Four was thieving animal. Intend to find Sea-Wyf.
> BISCUIT.

But, for whatever reason, Sea-Wyf was silent. And on Wednesday April 11, five weeks after the first appeal to her, this announcement was printed in the same column:

> PUBLISHER REQUIRED for war story of three men of authority and one woman adrift 14 weeks on float in Indian Ocean. Survivors parted with nicknames only and compact to forget. "Were they right?" theme. P.R. 14672.
> *Daily Telegraph* E.C. 4.

Two days later, that is to say as quickly as it would be practical for her to do so, the mysterious lady reacted in print:

> BISCUIT. Do not publish. Give me a
> week to think. SEA-WYF.

That seemed to alter Biscuit's mood again. On April 16 he wrote:

> SEA-WYF. Anything you ask—"even
> unto half my water ration." BISCUIT.

Exactly a week after the lady's first response, she asked a question:

> BISCUIT. Why do you insist on seeing
> me again? SEA-WYF.

The reply came promptly:

> SEA-WYF. *Amor omnia vincit*—I
> hope. BISCUIT.

But on April 27 there was another question:

> BISCUIT. If I agree to see you will you
> promise not to mention 14 weeks?
> SEA-WYF.

And on the same day, in the same column, there was also printed:

> BISCUIT TO LAURIE. Keep your
> nose out of this business.

Three days later Biscuit answered Sea-Wyf's question with:

> Yes. But hurry.

There followed a week's interval, and then:

> BISCUIT. Will pass through Berwick Market at 2 P.M., Thursday on assurance you will not speak or approach.

The immediate answer was:

> SEA-WYF. All's fair in love and war, but what is this? Never mind. I agree.
> BISCUIT.

That appeared on Wednesday. On the day of the rendezvous this was printed:

> SEA-WYF. Will provide escort today.
> UNDERGRADUATE.

But on the Saturday following Biscuit appealed:

> SEA-WYF. I did not see you in the market. Why did you not come?
> BISCUIT.

SEA∗WYF

She answered four days later:

> BISCUIT. I came. I saw you once more
> which was the thing I wanted. Re-
> member me as I was when the smoke
> appeared on the horizon. Good-by.
> SEA-WYF.

May 21 apparently brought the story to a close:

> SEA-WYF. With all my will but much
> against my heart. Good-by. BISCUIT.

There were two more announcements, but these were evidently inserted by outsiders who had followed the correspondence. The first exhorted Biscuit to continue his efforts. The second stated pontifically: "No, it is better as it is." On May 26 the *Daily Mirror* printed the story as it had appeared, and I believe that on about the same day a Paris newspaper did the same. But these were merely recapitulations. There was nothing new.

So far I have been strictly factual. Anyone who did not follow the story at the time, and is sufficiently curious, may check these announcements in the files at the *Daily Telegraph* office or the British Museum. I myself was absorbedly interested in them. No doubt this was at least partly due to my condition at the time. I don't think I had yet quite settled down after the war. I was doing a job which did not interest me. I used to talk vaguely about throwing everything up and farming an island or trying to get back into Polar exploration. But I really knew that nothing of that sort would bring the real freedom, meaning independence and self-satisfaction, which I needed. I was spending all my spare time writing. I called it filing at the bars. I had had several books and stories published. They had bought me holidays, some quite good holidays, but that was all. What I wanted to do was travel the world and write real-life adventure, and to do that really well. But without success I could not afford to travel, and without travel I could not succeed. I felt barren and rather hopeless.

That was my mood when I read the correspondence which is quoted above. Those tantalizingly brief announcements hinted at a romantic and exciting story. If only the people concerned would tell it to me I felt certain that I could make a first-class book of it. I would use what I knew of technique and their firsthand experience.

It must be difficult, to say the least, for someone who does not write to understand the urge of a writer. It is as strong and undisciplined as that of love yet intellectually more absorbing, (or perhaps it is still more independent of worldly wisdom and common sense.) Rather it is like the urge of a prospector, and indeed at the time I would have dug up those details as excitedly as a gold mine. I had a hunch that there was something well worth reading between those scanty lines. My interest took many practical forms. I tried hard and I thought ingeniously to become the author of that story. But everything went wrong. I missed chances. All my efforts ended in absurd, even humiliating little adventures. Or so it seemed at the time.

When the announcements ceased I attempted from the scant data to reconstruct the story on my own. But again without much success. And gradually as the months passed by, Sea-Wyf, Biscuit, Bulldog and Number Four receded from my thoughts and ambitions.

Then I had one of those strokes of luck which come to an author once in a lifetime. More than three years later I quite suddenly found myself in a position to write the whole story —on one condition. None of the characters should be recognizable in real life. It must be impossible for anyone to identify them. That meant that the story had to be created as fiction and even my own actions disguised. Therefore, although sailing as near as possible to the wind of truth, I have written what must please be read as a novel, and I may as well state now that I am not at liberty to answer any questions about it.

Having made that clear, and become the "I" of a story in which "the characters are entirely imaginary and bear no relation to any living person," I will start again at the begining.

CHAPTER TWO

SOMETHING holds me back from the risk of spending an extra minute at the office and whatever it is that goes on there. So on the morning of March 7, 1951, I was in the usual hurry. At the bottom of the moving staircase I heard the guard of the underground train shouting, "Mind the doors." I took the fixed steps four at a time, slipped and twisted my ankle. I hopped into a carriage as the automatic doors snapped shut.

Standing on one leg I looked round for a seat. They were all occupied. It must have been obvious from my face that I was in pain, but no one got up and invited me to sit down. Nobody noticed me. They read their newspapers. Swaying unconsciously to the jolting motion of the noisy train, pretty girls and middle-aged women, young men and old, were interested in nothing but the daily press.

Angrily I glanced at my own newspaper, which I had just bought and was grasping, still folded, in the hand I did not need for holding on.

That was when I read the first of Biscuit's announcements.

About a week later I heard the second commented on by two strangers in a bus. "Have returned with fatted calf . . ." They agreed it must have been put in by a Biblical society. Those charities had money to burn on publishing quotations.

The third announcement was discussed by three friends and myself on the first evening of a yachting week end at Burnham-on-Crouch. We guests had that Friday afternoon arrived from London, changed from city clothes to slacks and sweaters, cooked and eaten a real meal. Still comfortably at our moorings, waiting for the ebb, we were fogging the cabin with pipes and cigarettes. And the Skipper, our host, remarked in his drily humorous way that a lot of people were ready to pay money to give up smoking. Feeling tough we laughed at that. But the Skipper said he had noticed a number of Stop Smoking advertisements in the Agony Column of his newspaper.

We expressed surprise that so independent a person as himself read any newspaper in that much detail, and he admitted that since one cannot open a paper in a wind he read only the front and back pages. I asked him if he had seen Biscuit's appeals to Sea-Wyf. He had. One of my fellow guests had heard about them, but not the other. I read out that morning's announcement—"Am certain you are alive. Are you

afraid of the past or me." We discussed it. Henry Wooller
said it was a Stop Smoking advertisement. Sea-Wyf would
not have anything to do with him because she could not abide
the smell of tobacco. Charles Maynard said no, she had not
answered simply because, like himself, she took the *Daily
Mail*. But we agreed that if she did not read the *Telegraph*
she would surely have overheard the name "Sea-Wyf" and
pricked up her ears. Henry then suggested that the whole
thing was a practical joke. But that did not seem likely when
we worked out the cost, at least thirty-five shillings a time.
Charles had the romantic idea that the messages were in code
and addressed to members of a gang.

Then Henry who is a publisher chiefly concerned with
educational and scientific books remarked that he thought
a sea-wyf was some sort of fish. Was there a dictionary on
board? There wasn't. But the Skipper, who has read most
of what has been written about the sea, told us that sea-wyf
(which is pronounced sea-wife) was an old sailor's term for
a mermaid. As he said that his eyes lighted up, and he went
on, "There may be something worthwhile in this thing after
all. Ten to one it's a hoax or an advertisement, as you say. But
there is the other chance. Nobody ever believes anything
really good, what they would like to believe. Do you remember that fellow who offered pound notes for twopence
each in Regent Street and nobody stopped to buy them because they felt sure there must be a catch? That's the state
of mind most of us have got into. But Peter Fleming was

launched on his Brazilian adventure by answering an advertisement in the Agony Column of the *Times*. It's better to
risk making a fool of yourself than miss a chance."

I think that conversation started my more than logical interest in the suggested drama. I dare say this was largely
from association, a real-life week end which broke a trivial
work-a-day existence; or perhaps it was only because the
old Skipper's eyes had glowed with wisdom as he said that
people never believe anything really good—I don't know.
But I went back to London with my nostrils still tingling
from the tang of the sea—for we had sailed out into some
brisk equinoctial weather—and my mind full of a mermaid
who had come ashore and a man who was looking for her.
Sea-Wyf and Biscuit, and the other characters when they
appeared, became more real for me than the people who
hurried past me in the street or crowded into underground
trains.

In the middle of the week Biscuit announced to Sea-Wyf
that he intended to find her "by publishing story of fourteen
weeks and Number Four." I rang up Henry Wooller and
told him that his firm ought to get in touch with Biscuit
through the *Telegraph* and offer a contract for a book. He
said that sort of thing was not quite their line. I asked what
sort of line he thought "fourteen weeks and Number Four"
was, and he answered: "Well, we don't offer our contracts
blind, you know, old boy."

During the next couple of weeks Bulldog entered the

scene and wrangled with Biscuit about the ethics of resurrecting the story. I read of the compact, I got the date of whatever had happened—nine years previously, or 1942, and I learned that Number Four was a thieving animal.

One day it occurred to me to go down to Fleet Street and see if there was anything to be discovered from the *Daily Telegraph*. The Classified Advertisement Department is an enormous U-shaped room full of very young and often very pretty girls. The manager, a man, has a glass case to himself. He could not have been nicer. He told me that he had had a number of other queries about Biscuit and Sea-Wyf, and the answer was that any announcement which was properly sent in and paid for, and which was not of course objectionable in any way, was inserted when space permitted. Naturally I could if I wished try to get in touch with Biscuit through the newspaper. I had not the face to ask if I might see one of the original letters, and the manager did not actually say whether he knew the real names of the correspondents himself. But he let me understand that names are confidential when an advertiser wishes to be anonymous.

As I walked away through the U-shaped room it struck me that one of its busy inhabitants must have dealt with the original letters and therefore should know the addresses if not the true identities of Biscuit and Bulldog, and that the wholehearted thing to do was to invite those thirty or forty young ladies out to dinner one after the other and try to wheedle the confidence out of them. But I decided not to do that.

The next event was the "Publisher Required . . ." advertisement which appeared on April 11. Although it concluded with a box number instead of a name it was obviously inserted by Biscuit. I was waiting in Henry's office when he arrived there that Wednesday morning.

I had chosen Henry not because I thought Ivor Meredith & Co. was the most suitable firm to publish such a story but because I believed I would stand a better chance of persuading him to do what I wanted than anybody else. I wanted him to answer the advertisement, get in touch with Biscuit, partly—to discover as much as possible about the story and partly—to be frank—that I myself might later have a chance to meet the participants. It took a lot of doing. Henry twisted and turned and promised to speak to his partners at the next conference. But he could not deny that he had nothing to lose by asking for an interview with Biscuit before any rival publisher did so, and in any case I think he realized there was only one way to get rid of me from his office. By eleven o'clock in the morning a reply-paid telegram, duly franked, had been personally handed in to the Classified Advertisement Department for forwarding to whatever postal address P. R. 14672 might stand for. And I went to my office an hour and a half late, too preoccupied to be able to think of a good excuse.

In the middle of the afternoon Henry rang me up. He sounded pleased with himself.

"I've had an answer to my wire," he said.

"What?"

" 'Will meet you privately in Duke Street Gardens W. 1 noon tomorrow. Biscuit.' "

"Where are Duke Street Gardens?" I asked.

"Between Oxford Street and Grosvenor Square."

"But there aren't any gardens there," I said.

"They are marked on the map. I've just looked them up," Henry answered.

I inquired if Biscuit had given any information as to how he could be recognized.

"No," Henry answered. "I've read you the whole wire."

"How do you think you'll recognize him?"

"I don't know."

"Shall I go with you?" I asked.

"No, definitely not. He says 'privately,' and I don't want to start negotiations on the wrong foot. We don't do that sort of thing in Ivor Meredith."

"Well, lunch with me afterwards at the R. A. C. and tell me all about it," I said.

Directly I got away from my office that evening I went to reconnoiter the rendezvous. It was not at all what I expected. Presumably there was once a patch of green between Duke Street and its parallel Balderton Street. But Progress has been at work. Now the Gardens are the flat roof of a semi-submerged depot or works of the London Electricity Board. They are about fifty yards by twenty in area, have a stone bowl of stagnant water in the middle, a few scattered seats and a balustrade. But there is not one blade of vegetable green. The Gardens are approached by a flight of steps at each of the four corners. At the head of each stairway is a notice:

DUKE STREET GARDENS

Bylaws

The garden is open to the public from 9 A.M. till sunset until further notice.

No idle person or persons in an intoxicated, unclean or verminous condition is allowed in the garden. . . .

No speech, address, performance, recitation or representation may be given.

The following acts are prohibited in the garden: Games, brawling, fighting, quarreling, gambling, betting, playing with cards or dice, shouting, singing, the practice of gymnastics, climbing the trees, railings or balustrade. . . .

Any person injuring the trees, shrubs, plants, seats, fountain or any part of the garden, or committing a breach of any of the above Bylaws will be prosecuted.

BY ORDER.

Reading this, I reverted for a moment to early fears that the whole thing might be a complicated practical joke. For if a rather precious young publisher were to go round asking everybody in the Garden if they were Biscuit it seemed highly probable that at least one of the by-laws would be broken. But very likely Biscuit had not read the notice—everybody does not find the same fascination in bureaucratic language. And there could be quite other reasons for choosing this rendezvous. The place was just about ideal for what presumably was Biscuit's purpose. It was sufficiently small and little frequented—at least before the lunch hour, I supposed—for two strangers having the same purpose to discover each other with the minimum of fuss. The wooden seats were far enough apart to be beyond earshot, while anybody standing about in the open space between would be conspicuous. From street level it would be impossible to see anyone up there who was not actually leaning on the balustrade, while Biscuit could leave by any of the four stairways and disappear in crowded streets within a matter of seconds. I had to renounce a plan, which I am afraid had been at the back of my mind, of eavesdropping or at least observing at the interview.

So there was nothing to do but wait—through an evening and a night and a morning—until Henry arrived for lunch at the R. A. C.

I heard him before I saw him, for he has a rather penetrating voice. He was greeting the head porter whom he seemed to know well. I waved and he came up the steps towards me three at a time. He was looking, as he always does, as if he had just had a bath, haircut and shampoo. His round face is absurdly young, his large eyes accentuated by unusually large spectacles. The only hint that he is over thirty is that his hair has receded from his forehead.

"Sorry to keep you waiting, old boy," he said.

"In this case you are forgiven because I suppose it means you have something to tell me."

"Yes, I have. But shall we go straight in? I must get back to the office rather soon—Wednesday conference."

"What was he like?" I asked as soon as we were seated.

"Not what I expected," Henry said.

"What did you expect?"

"I don't know exactly. But all that talk of home at last and the fatted calf, I'd thought he must have found gold in Australia—that sort of person."

"But he wasn't."

"No, not at all."

"Well, what *was* he like?"

You have to be patient with Henry. He had broken off to hold an earnest conversation with the waitress about the choice of foods on the menu. When that important business was settled he turned back to me and asked:

"Can you describe a person, I mean unless he is odd in some way? I can't. Nor can the police for that matter when they want to find a murderer or something. Height about five feet ten, average build, age forty to forty-five, blue eyes, complexion sallow, clean shaven—"

"Is this Biscuit?" I asked.

"Yes, it's accurate."

"So it would be for a dozen men in this room," I said.

"That's exactly what I mean," Henry answered in the tone of one who has made a good point.

"What color was his hair?" I asked.

"Never saw the gentleman with 'is 'at off," Henry's serious face suddenly broke into a schoolboy smile. "Do you know that story? Queen Mary was going round a maternity hospital. She saw a baby with bright red hair and asked the mother if the father's was the same. And she said—"

"For Heaven's sake stick to the point. Don't you take this seriously? Do you think Biscuit is a hoaxer?"

"I don't think he is a hoaxer," he answered. "I asked him to give me a general sketch of his story—I could not discuss publication otherwise. He did, and it rang true, extraordinary though it was. But, no, I don't take it seriously."

"Why not?"

"It wouldn't make a book."

"Please tell it to me," I said.

Henry was carefully taking the bones out of his fried sole and I had to wait some time for his reply.

"Biscuit was on a ship which I gathered was trying to get away from the Japs. The time, I think, was the beginning of 1942, and they were sailing westward across the Indian Ocean when they were torpedoed or struck a mine—anyway the ship sank very quickly. Everybody except these four was evidently killed or soon died. But Biscuit and Co. somehow survived on a raft."

"For fourteen weeks?" I asked.

"Yes, that's one of the weak points of the story," Henry said. "He told me that you could not expect details at seventeen and six a line, and he more or less admitted that what he'd put in was primarily bait for a publisher. I didn't like that. No, I can't see it as a book."

"I still can't see your objection," I said.

"Look at it this way. Of course before anything went to the printer we would have to check the facts. If they didn't prove true the thing would be out, naturally. But even if they were, as I believe is the case, wouldn't it be too much of a good thing, or rather of a bad thing?"

"What on earth do you mean?"

Henry fixed his round eyes on me.

"Fourteen weeks—ninety-eight days and nights on a raft. What sort of a book would that make? One bit of sea is exactly like the next. Think of the repetitions. And another thing—three men and a woman—there's no privacy on a raft, you know. It might make a horrible short story. But not a book."

"A spot of horror is not unsalable I should have thought," I murmured. But Henry went on speaking as if he had not heard me.

"Biscuit refused to give his real name. And the man who calls himself Bulldog does not want publication—there was that thing about a compact. My firm never touches anything unless the legal position is perfectly clean and clear."

"You are very cautious," I said.

"One has to be. Believe me, there are quite enough financial dangers in the publishing profession without risking thousands of pounds on damages or having to withdraw a book. It might be worth the risk if I knew the fellow could write, but I don't. Horror may be salable, as you say, but it has to be damned well done."

"Then how did you leave it?" I asked.

"That we would be very glad to see his manuscript if he cared to send it in."

"And with that you parted?"

"Yes."

Since Biscuit's "Intend to find you by publishing . . ." announcement, my hopes of discovering what had happened had seesawed up and down. At that moment they were as low as they could be.

CHAPTER THREE

HENRY spent the rest of the meal talking about the business visit to New York he was to make in a fortnight's time, and while he was doing so I decided to write to Biscuit myself. My hopes soared up again as I composed the letter. Back in my office I typed it out on a sheet of my own notepaper.

It ran as follows:

Dear Sir,

My object in addressing you is to offer my help. I believe you would find me a useful collaborator when it comes to writing your adventures and making a contract for the MS.

I know the sort of thing you must have gone through—the stark danger and hardship broken only by monotony. There is a great deal of public interest in stories like yours. But if I may say so they need careful treatment.

It so happens that I have had some experience of the technique required to prepare material of that sort to the best advantage. As far as money is concerned you need not hesitate. I would agree to any reasonable arrangement.

Before taking any other steps, I do most seriously suggest that you should get in touch with me at the above address, for I am sure that you will find it worth while.

Yours faithfully,

It seemed to me that that ought to allay any doubt which Henry might have caused. There were no frills about the letter, certainly, but I believed it was the sort of thing that would appeal to the sort of person I thought Biscuit to be. For in spite of Henry's negative description I had a definite picture of him in my mind—an Elizabethan adventurer born out of his time.

I addressed the envelope to the box number and posted it at once.

At nine next evening my telephone bell rang. A man's voice inquired who I was. I told him and asked the same question. "Biscuit," he said.

I was taken aback, but he went on speaking in a drawling voice with a slight lilt in it. He said he had rung up earlier in the evening but had been told that I was not yet in. He thanked me for my letter. He said he did not expect it would be necessary for him to ask help, but it was good of me to make the offer.

I was surprised at his remarkable politeness. After all, my offer to a perfect stranger had verged on the impertinent.

Then he said,

"Had you heard anything of this story before? I mean before my first announcement in the *Telegraph?*"

"No," I said, puzzled.

"Do you know anything about Sea-Wyf?"

"No, nothing."

"You give me your word that is true?"

"Yes—yes, certainly."

"The final sentence of your letter only referred to literary help?"

"Yes, of course."

"Thank you," he said in a suddenly brisk voice, "Good-by."

For some moments after he had rung off I sat still holding the telephone in my hand. Then I replaced it with a crash which made the cat wake up. What a slow-witted fool I was! Obviously Biscuit had taken the trouble to ring me up only because in my letter I had unwittingly suggested that I knew something about Sea-Wyf. There would have been no need to tell an actual falsehood, but if I had been a little less definite in my denials I might have arranged a meeting, and anything could have come out of that. *Esprit d'escalier!*

I sat late that night beside the open window, listening to the noise of traffic, seeing beyond it in my mind's eye a lonely raft in mid ocean . . .

A bus accelerated with the metallic blowing of a trumpeting elephant. A sports car growled, impatient in low gear. Another changed down with the snapping snarl of a charging lion. The shrill alarm note of an ambulance told that one of the great beasts had made a kill. Beyond this darkest England was the brilliant sunshine of the Indian Ocean, with floating on its water a hint of real-life romance which drifted farther and farther away. For I was condemned to remain in the jungle, rooting for food all day and going down to the drinking pool at night.

This seemed to be confirmed next morning by Sea-Wyf's announcement: "Do not publish. Give me a week to think." I was not surprised that neither Henry Wooller nor I received any other communication from Biscuit.

SEA≠WYF

From April 13 until May 7, more than three weeks, Sea-Wyf was asking questions, Biscuit agreeing to her condition and exhorting her to meet him. Only one announcement needs comment here. That is the one which appeared on the same day as Sea-Wyf's request for a promise "not to mention 14 weeks." I mean, "Biscuit to Laurie. Keep your nose out of this business."

Was Laurie some outside person who knew at least a little of the story and was making trouble? Or was he only another inquisitive stranger like myself? I could only guess. But it was clear enough that I would have to be careful how I poked my own nose in.[1]

The climax of the series of announcements came when Sea-Wyf stated that she would pass through Berwick Market at two o'clock on the afternoon of May 10. This, I felt sure, would be my last chance of seeing any of the people concerned. But I also realized it was a slender one. If Henry could have accompanied me there would have been a reasonable hope of success. But Henry, exasperating as ever, was by now in New York.

I went to Berwick Street at twenty minutes to two that Thursday afternoon. The market consists of a hundred and fifty yards stretch, part of a pedestrian thoroughfare from the busy heart of Soho and Oxford Street in the north, to

---

[1] To save the reader any unnecessary puzzlement I will explain here what I only discovered myself much later, that this announcement was not inserted by Biscuit. I have never discovered who put it in, or why, but in any case it has nothing to do with the story.

Shaftesbury Avenue and Piccadilly Circus in the south.
The narrow street is fringed by shops, and all day long it is
more than half obstructed by a double line of stalls and bar-
rows. These just leave the pavements clear, providing a
yard-wide passage on each side and another about two yards
wide in the middle of the street. But the word passage gives
a false impression for there are besides the buying crowd,
and saleswomen, rarely less than two to a stall, who take up
a good deal of room as well as making a lot of noise. " 'Ave
no fear, Abel's 'ere" is a typical slogan, and there is a continuous chorus of East End wit. You are being offered at
bargain prices ladies' handbags, fruit, vegetables, toilet goods,
costume jewelry, plants for the garden, nylon stockings,
lengths of cloth, fish or flowers or almost anything else
which can be thought of. Particularly in the middle of the
day people stroll slowly through the market in both direc-
tions or stop to examine, buy or bargain. Others have
business to do in the fringing shops, and quite a number are
merely trying to get through Berwick Street as quickly as
possible.

Waiting for the hour to strike I considered what my plan
should be. My best if not only chance of recognizing Sea-
Wyf and Biscuit would be to see them actually meeting each
other. Biscuit's expression when he caught sight of the woman he had been so earnestly looking for must certainly be
striking. The very fact that he was not to speak or approach
would make his face the more expressive. And Sea-Wyf too
could scarcely fail to show emotion. But I had no idea where

in that hundred and fifty yards stretch this might take place. Should I stand still or move up and down? I tried to make up my mind what to do—and did nothing.

Then I caught sight of a young man in flannel trousers and a tweed coat. His eyes were bright and purposeful, his chin set. In one hand he carried a copy of the *Daily Telegraph* and in the other a heavy-headed stick. I started, then relaxed. Undoubtedly this was the undergraduate who that morning had announced in the paper that he would provide an escort in the market. I watched him until, within a few seconds, he disappeared in the crowd. I felt that I ought to follow his energetic example—but instead I remained where I was trusting to luck.

It was two o'clock by now. I stood on the pavement between two stalls where I could at least see right across the street. I waited for five minutes.

The undergraduate passed me again. His expression was less like that of a knight-errant than it had been. He looked slightly foolish. But I was relieved to see him again. He had searched the market as a dog searches a covert, and found nothing. I was right to stand still.

While the undergraduate was still in sight I noticed that someone else, on the other side of the road but quite close to me, was also looking at him intently. And immediately I felt certain that the other person was Biscuit.

To avoid giving myself away I turned aside and became interested in the nearest stall. Unfortunately it was of women's underclothes, and the stall keeper began telling me what a bargain the things were. To shut him up I bought something. And all the time I was watching the man on the other side of the road. He had stationed himself in a place where he had a good view of the passers by—as Biscuit would do. He was of medium height and build, with a sallow complexion, what I could see of it. He fitted Henry's description. He was wearing a long country mackintosh with the high collar turned up, obscuring his chin and part of his cheeks. On his head was a felt hat with the rim turned down. But I was less interested in those details than in the fact that he was still waiting. In one particular at least the mysterious Sea-Wyf did not differ from the rest of her sex. She was late for the appointment.

I felt perfectly at ease now, and confident. I strolled across the road as if interested in other stalls and had a close look at the man. Without forcing myself on his attention I could not see any more of his face. But I noticed that below his point-to-point mackintosh he was wearing dark city trousers and black shoes. I would have liked to make him speak but did not think it worth the risk. Instead I retired to a safe distance and continued to observe him. One thing struck me. Although he looked both up and down the street he was generally looking up it, northwards, sometimes rising on tiptoe to see more clearly. I wondered why he should think it more likely that Sea-Wyf would come from that direction.

As the minutes passed and nothing happened I tried to remember what lay between the market and Oxford Street. I knew Soho fairly well from exploring its restaurants and wandering about its curious continental streets. Besides the food places there was Foyles' bookshop and a couple of publishers. There were a number of fashion houses and women's wholesale clothiers. There were a hospital or two, at least one very large garage, a minor B. B. C. office where I had once given a school broadcast, and any number of film company offices.

At quarter to three I was still engaged in this unrewarding mental exercise when the man began to walk northwards. He kept his head high, peering above the shoulders of those in front of him, as if he were following somebody.

His start had taken me unaware, and he was twenty yards or more in front of me. Although the crowds had thinned there were far too many people about for me to see whom he was following. I moved after him at a cautious distance.

I kept him in sight to the northern end of the market where there is a crossroads and one is among vehicles again. I was afraid that I might lose him there. But he halted on the pavement edge. I stopped behind him, trying to follow the direction of his eyes.

He stood in the same position for perhaps three minutes. Then he hailed a passing taxi and drove off towards the city. There was a satisfied expression on his face.

I returned to my office where I got into trouble for being so late. A flap and flurry was going on about something or other. As I hung up my coat the thing I had bought in the market fell out of the pocket onto the floor.

Altogether it was a bad day.

CHAPTER FOUR

No doubt the Skipper was right, that it is better to make a fool of yourself than miss a chance. But I had done both. Of course the meeting had taken place before, (at about 2:15) I saw that man in a mackintosh. Any woman would be punctual on an occasion like that. Why had I not made a plan beforehand and stuck to it? Why had I taken it for granted that the man was Biscuit? He might have been a detective, or a businessman filling in time before an appointment, or some person interested in an entirely different sort of woman. Strange things, or at least unsavory things, happen in the streets of Soho.

Then came Biscuit's announcement asking Sea-Wyf why she had not come.

So the man I saw might have been Biscuit after all . . .

Then Sea-Wyf said that she had come, and that she had seen him. What could have happened to change her out of all recognition in those nine years?

But Biscuit accepted her good-by, and there was nothing more.

I continued to do the same job—and three years went by. It is difficult to give an impression of that interval of time because so little that I can remember happened in its course. Most people must have noticed that when one's time hangs heavily and seems to go on so slowly, it yet somehow or other is racing by faster than ever. The days crawl, but when you think of some seemingly recent event you discover with a shock that it happened a couple of years before. Our days, I suppose, are like those paper folding cartons. If one fills them they are bulky things in the storehouse. But if they are merely fitted together and left empty, they squash each other flat again and take up very little room indeed.

I continued, as I have said, to do the same job. I had lost the initiative which would have got me out of it.

The Skipper did try to get me out of it. My occasional week ends of sailing with him were the high lights of my existence. He was such a sure, drily amusing person. Chiefly he was sure. He knew just what he was doing, which was what he wanted to do. He lived on a twenty-five ton ketch. He had no base. Sometimes he played about an English port. But as a rule he was engaged on a passage of six months or more. He used to send me laconic postcards, (picture post-cards when they were available). "You ought to see the giant tortoises on St. Helena," or—from the Galápagos— "Having a wonderful time. Wish you were here."

The occasions when I could do a few days' sailing with him were naturally rare. But when they occurred we enjoyed each other's company as much as the exercise. Although he was twenty years older than I, we could wrangle as cheerfully as contemporaries. He was always telling me to give up the job I complained about and join him on a long passage. I answered that I had responsibilities and that he was an unprincipled old ruffian—which made his eyes sparkle and his shoulders shrug as if I had paid him a compliment. But we had more serious conversations too. He seemed to have read everything while the tiller was lashed. Of course he had read all the Biscuit-Bulldog-Sea-Wyf correspondence. What struck me was his point of view. To me the suggested adventure was, I suppose, akin to escape fiction—something to daydream about. To him it was in no way unrelated to reasonable life. We might have been talking about three men and a girl who had come down the Thames in a punt.

"Wreck survivor stories are always interesting," he said. "It's amazing what the human animal can stand when it has to. Bligh of the *Bounty*, and then only about twenty years ago the *Travessa*. Her crew did seventeen hundred miles in open boats. That was in the Indian Ocean. We must explore the Indian Ocean some time. You'll come with me then, won't you?"

"If I can get away," I said.

"If you can get away!"

He reached behind him on the shelf which ran, shoulder high, round both sides of the cabin, and took down the *Southern Indian Ocean Pilot*, 1946. He lapped through the pages, now and then waving away his own tobacco smoke with his left hand and reading out a passage about some tropical harbor, or a sandbank marked by a conspicuous casuarina tree or some lovely coral island.

The yacht stirred restlessly at her moorings, but she was no more restless than I.

We had another conversation six months later. The Skipper arrived at my office, short, broad, sunburned, and took me out to lunch. Over the roast beef he said, "You have got to sail with me this time."

"Where?"

"To the Indian Ocean."

"Why?"

"Why? Biscuit and Sea-Wyf."

"Biscuit and Sea-Wyf?"

"Don't say you've forgotten."

"Of course not. But—"

"What?"

"Well, that happened—let me see—eleven years ago. And it's a huge great Ocean. There isn't a chance of you finding any trace."

The Skipper laughed so much that I began to feel annoyed.

"What's so funny?"

"Nothing. I was admiring your singleness of purpose. I'm not really going all the way to the Indian Ocean to solve the mystery of Sea-Wyf and Biscuit."

"Then why?"

"Because it is the best ocean for cruising—much pleasanter than the Atlantic. I don't know why so few yachtsmen try it—or why I haven't tried it before myself. If you pick your route and season you can have fair winds all the way. And remember those coral lagoons, dazzling white sand, coconuts and casuarina trees. Come with me."

"I can't. They wouldn't keep my job open."

"To hell with your job. You've been bored with it for seven years."

"If I gave it up now those years would be wasted. As it is . . ."

I wanted to accept very much indeed, but I knew it would be wrong.

The Skipper sat smiling at me, with affection but a hint of pity too which I found most aggravating.

"Your ambition is to be a successful author—and you sit in London," he said. "You want to write real-life adventure —and you will not even risk losing your job. Be honest with yourself. Your devotion to the Sea-Wyf story is an excuse for doing nothing. Even if it did drop into your lap, what could you make of it? A second-hand botch up of someone else's misadventure. Never mind about Sea-Wyf and Biscuit. Come with me and you can write a far better story all your own, blazing with local color and first impressions. Look, we might follow a course like this—"

He took out a pencil and drew a sketch map of the Indian Ocean on the tablecloth, dotting in the islands. I could see it all in his description.

"Skipper, please, don't!" I said. "I can't go with you. I have to earn a living."

"All right, all right. We'll say no more about it."

He dashed his pencil across and across his map of the Indian Ocean, crossing it out.

I did not see the Skipper again before he sailed. But during the following months—the late winter and into the spring of 1954—I received letters or postcards—from Gibraltar, Port Said and Aden. Then, at longer intervals, he wrote from one or another of the islands of the Indian Ocean. What fascinating names they had— Silhouette, Curieuse, Coetivity, Providence and Cerf. Only twice did he make a reference to the Sea-Wyf story. The first was facetious—"Thought I saw the raft today, but it turned out to be the Flying Dutchman . . ." His second reference concerned a research vessel which he had come across. She was engaged, he said, in a systematic tour of all the inhabited and uninhabited islands which dot the western quarter of the Indian Ocean, many of which had not been operated for copra and turtle fishing since the beginning of the war, or since private leases from the Seychelles and Mauritius government had run out. "You might have signed on with her since you would not sail with me. Then you would have had a paid job and another excellent chance of discovering your story or a still better one," the Skipper wrote.

It was a wet and dismal summer in England. Walking through crowded streets or dripping parks I saw continuously a little white yacht sailing gaily through the dazzling blue. I heard the breakers on the coral reef, smelt the vegetation, touched the sun-warmed sand. I had felt so self-righteous about refusing the Skipper's invitation and re-maining at my desk. But had I been right to miss such a rare chance of action? They also serve who only stand and wait. Yes, but they serve double faults.

I was in that half-romantic, half-cynical and altogether unsatisfied state of mind when my eye was caught by a picture in the gossip column of an evening paper.

CHAPTER FIVE

I MANAGED to fold back the page and study the picture. (I was one of the five standing passengers in a bus at the time). It was of a man with a shotgun under his arm and it was captioned, "M. P. inherits." The man was wearing a mackintosh with the collar turned up—a not uncommon sight that August. Yet there was something about him . . . .

Being in a gossip column, it took a little time to find the paragraph which referred to the picture. Then I read:

> Mr. Jonathan Natham M.P., has inherited from his uncle, the millionaire shipowner Herbert Natham, the estate of Alata in the Isle of Skye. Natham, who is a barrister, tells me that he hopes to hold shooting parties there next year. The Jacobean castle has been completely restored and is luxuriously furnished, but the estate suffered seriously both from neglect and vermin during the war. Natham is as interested in woodcock as in grouse. An accomplished amateur artist, he uses for his brush paint the traditional woodcock's pinfeather.

The paragraph did nothing to confirm the impression which the photograph had caused, but I went to see Henry Wooller at once.

I found him changing to go to the theater. I showed him the picture and asked him if he knew who it was.

"No," he said and went on tying his tie.

"Please look carefully. Have you ever seen that man?"

Henry took another glance. "I can't say I recognize him. Should I?"

"I believe you saw him three and a quarter years ago."

"Three and a quarter years ago? Good Lord, where?"

"In Duke Street Gardens."

"What do you mean? What?—"

"Could that be Biscuit?"

He grabbed the paper from me and studied it for some time.

"Why on earth should Mr. Jonathan Natham be Biscuit?" he asked.

"Never mind about that. Could he be the man you met in Duke Street Gardens?"

Henry stared at the picture. "It doesn't strike a chord, old boy. But that photo must have been taken in the rain. You can hardly see the face."

"Was Biscuit wearing a mackintosh like that when you met him?"

Henry frowned. "I don't think he was wearing any sort of overcoat."

"What kind of suit?"

"How could anybody—"

"Well, go as far as this at any rate—could that man be Biscuit?"

Henry flicked a brush over his evening clothes and admired himself in the mirror.

"It could in that he has two legs and two arms, but I don't

suppose for a moment it is. Damn it, one can't possibly remember after all that time. I meet so many people. Sorry,
old boy, I must dash or I'll be late."

I was not put off. I rang up the art room of the newspaper
and was told that the picture came from an agency. I rang
up the agency, and at lunch time next day collected a print
on glossy paper. It was much clearer, of course, but it did
not prove anything. It was almost full face whereas the as-
pect I remembered was the profile. I put the photograph in
the drawer of my desk and kept glancing at it when I ought
to have been doing something else.

That evening I went to my club and looked up Natham in
Who's Who. In a long list of achievements and activities
there was nothing about the Far East. But if he had gone out
there at the beginning of the war on some tour or brief of
Commission would that have been worth inclusion? Or would
he in the circumstances have wanted it to be included? I was
not convinced that I was wrong. All the same, I doubt if I
would actually have done anything about it except (this is
the immoral way Fate works) that I met Kenneth Meade
with whom I had soldiered in the war. What we said to each
other during the next three hours I can't remember but we
had a very good dinner and when I got home I wrote this
letter:

Dear Mr. Natham,
   I am wondering if after this long interval you do not think
that the story of the fourteen weeks and Number Four ought
to be published. Obviously you have not time to write it your-

self. But I will gladly do that work. I think you will agree that I am the best man to do it. I would treat the matter with good taste and judgement—just as it should be treated. You need not be afraid that I would overstress any of the unpleasant aspects. To remind you of my long and intimate interest I enclose my former letter about which you remember we spoke, you saying that you would call upon me when the time was ripe.

I put into the envelope a carbon of the letter I had written on April 11, 1951. Then I went out and posted it at once for fear that next morning I might think better of it. If I were wrong in my guess, Natham would think I was merely mad and put the letter in the wastepaper basket. But if I were right, impressed by my knowing his name, he would answer it at once.

I was right to the extent that next morning I regretted having posted it. When I read the copy which was lying by my typewriter I was appalled. For days I was half afraid to look at my mail. But no letter came from Jonathan Natham, and after a week or so I began to forget about the incident and to think instead about my holiday which was due to start at the beginning of September and which I had not yet arranged.

And then one evening when I returned to my house the maid told me that a gentleman was waiting for me in my study. I asked who it was.

"He didn't give a name. He said you would be expecting him," she answered.

When I opened the door a man in black formal clothes

was sitting in the armchair with his hat and gloves on his knees. He got up and introduced himself as Jonathan Natham —although that was unnecessary—and apologized for his intrusion. He had had business in the neighborhood, he said, and had taken the opportunity to call on me.

I let him make these conventional remarks while I studied him. The parts of his face which I had not seen before were the sharp chin and the high, narrow forehead. His hair was dark and his complexion pale, very pale for one who had recently been in Skye. His mouth, I now noticed, was a thin straight line. He was of medium build and middle-aged, but I thought Henry had been wrong in saying that Biscuit had no particular feature to help description. He ought to have recognized that this was a legal face, most characteristic of all the professions—hard, keen, clever. At least I had thought in the market that he might be a detective, which was somewhere in the right direction.

I took his hat and gloves and invited him to sit down again. I was thinking fast. I was determined not to let this opportunity slip by. My best line, I thought, was to behave as if his coming to my home like this were the most natural thing in the world. I offered him a drink which he refused.

"Shall we get down to business? I came to ask you the meaning of your letter," he said.

"I am sorry if I did not make myself clear," I answered. "I happen to feel rather strongly that your story ought to be published—"

"What story?"

"The *Telegraph* Agony Column story—of what happened when you were on that float in the Indian Ocean."

"I see," he said, and paused. Then he shot at me, "And why *ought* that story to be published?"

He was speaking aggressively, sharp and hard, but I was not put off. The fact that he had come to see me proved that my guess had been right.

"It ought to be published for a number of reasons," I said. "The account would be useful to any one else who might be shipwrecked, for instance. But, chiefly, a great deal of public interest was aroused when that correspondence appeared in the *Telegraph*. That interest should be satisfied. Otherwise people may find an unpleasant reason for your silence. And it is always possible that an inaccurate account might be published by somebody else."

"What exactly do you know of this story already?" he asked.

"Quite a lot. For instance, the ship was bringing evacuees from the Far East in 1942. It was sunk in the middle of the Indian Ocean and all except the four who have been mentioned lost their lives. The float drifted with the Trade Winds—."

"Tell me this," he interrupted, "how do you suppose that I can help you?"

His manner was positively rude, but I pretended not to notice this. I had never felt more confident. And I guessed from the tenseness of his expression that he was nervous.

"Help me? By telling me the whole story, Mr. Biscuit," I said.

For fully a minute after that he remained looking at me straight in the face without moving at all. Then in a tone which was very quiet yet harder than ever, he said: "So that is the explanation. You imagine I am Biscuit."

"Imagine? But—of course—"

"Have you seen me before?" he asked.

"Yes. In the Berwick Market."

"That is possible. I am a bit of an artist and whenever I can I go to odd corners to study London types. Have you ever heard me speak?"

"No—yes I have—on the telephone. You rang me up."

"So you remember my voice?"

"It was over three years ago. How could I remember after all that time?" I said. But I felt myself blushing because those were almost exactly the words Henry had used. Henry had not thought the man in the picture was Biscuit. And now it came back to me that Biscuit had had a drawling voice. This man did anything but drawled.

He saw my discomfiture and struck like a snake.

"It is a good thing in civilized society— in uncivilized society too, I dare say—to make sure of your facts before you start building stories on them. I happen to have read one or two of your books, sir. I found them good entertainment. But I do not intend to become one of your characters, the plaything of your imagination, made to dance for the entertainment of others. If you try anything like that I warn you that the book will not pay. The balance will be very heavily on the other side. We do not tolerate libel in this country. I shall keep the remarkably suggestive letter and enclosure which you sent me. I shall keep them, shall we say, as a guarantee of good faith. Do you understand me?"

"Yes," I said. "Yes, I do."

CHAPTER SIX

TEN days after this incident, on Wednesday, September 1, the telephone bell rang on my desk and the operator said, "Hold on, Skye wants you."

It was Natham, and amazingly polite. He began apologizing for his behavior at our meeting. He said he had a great favor to request, but might he first ask me one or two questions.

"Can you do shorthand?" he inquired.

Surprised, I said yes, I could. I had been trained as a reporter. Then he asked:

"How long does it take you to write a book?"

I answered that with fiction it was impossible to say because it depended so much on inspiration. But with a factual matter, if one's ideas were clear, it was possible to go straight ahead, and I knew I was capable of many thousands of words a day.

That appeared to satisfy him.

"I wonder if you could possibly take a long week end and come up to Alata," he said. "I can't explain over the phone, but it is important. You will find it worth your while."

I said that my holiday was due to start on the Friday evening but that if I could start earlier I would. I took down the necessary details and rang off.

My holiday plans had not amounted to anything very much, but after those preliminary questions of Natham's I would have thrown up anything, and it did not overtax my imagination to get permission to start early. I sent Natham a wire and caught the night train from King's Cross next evening.

The railway journey from London towards the Isle of Skye must be as long as any in the British Isles. We got into Edinburgh in the small hours of the morning and shunted off some coaches—which woke me from my uncomfortable doze. The route northwards was new to me, and I was as excited as a schoolboy on holiday in any case. I got up and stood in the corridor, grasping the brass rail.

It was an almost clear night, with a few great black clouds which were just beginning to change to a lighter color. The moon rode smoothly and easily over a changing countryside, keeping up with the train as a dolphin accompanies a ship. First there was the rolling country to Queensferry. Then, rumbling over the great bridge where the rivet-studded pillars flick by one after another, there was the Firth of Forth, a lovely silver gray. Beyond, it was beginning to be dawn and I made out the woods and the villages, with only one window lighted here and there. And then we were entering the Highlands, and the blue smoke of croft chimneys rose shimmering into the morning air. Later, the great, flat-topped, purple Cairngorm Mountains sprawled sleepily in the bright morning sun.

I shaved and breakfasted at Inverness, and then the train went on, following a difficult route slowly yet confidently, as a guide does in the mountains. We passed pine coppices which sheltered white hunting lodges, and small stations made of planks, and lochs and bracken and gorse and heather. Occasionally there was a pile of stones and a bulldozer where the Hydro-Electric had been at work, harnessing the rivers, but for the most part it was wild, untamed Highland country. Then we came upon a long arm of sea, the ocean, and at last we were at the Kyle of Loch Alsh.

I went on board the little ferry ship which was due to start in half an hour. It did not start for two. There was a bull, a fine fellow with great horns, angry, puzzled eyes, and the lather of disapproval on his cheeks, who would not go on board though porters and small boys prodded him with sticks and tugged upon his halter. There was also a flock of sheep which were just as unwilling to embark. Finally there was a metal container about the size of an average dining room to be carried as deck cargo. The crane picked it up and tried to put it down here and there. But it would not fit, and swung about banging into things and generally behaving as obstinately in its inanimate way as the animals had done. The Captain, a philosophic Scot, smoked his pipe. In due time we started.

No one who has not made that voyage of a few hours can guess the magic of it. It is all sea and islands, and mountains which start up out of nowhere, and misty distance. You cannot tell how far away anything is in the sun and mist and showers. You are not quite certain that what you see is real. You have glimpses of enormous masses of rock, but the next moment they are swallowed up by clouds which have raced across the water to devour them. Then, when the sun blazes out with a rainbow, they are there again yet different, silver instead of black. You are being taken into a northern fairyland. To me it seemed that anything might happen.

We came into Portree harbor and the spell was nearly broken by all the business of shouting and throwing ropes from the ship and running about on the quay. (This is done by ships with engines only to impress the passengers, for when a rope misses—as it did on this occasion—it does not matter at all). But I had time to look at the port—the fishing boats, the lines of little houses and, up on the left, a cluster of pine trees rising above rocks, a place where the Greeks would certainly have built a temple if they had come to Skye.

Natham had told me on the phone that a car with a certain registration number would be waiting for me. Sure enough it was. I asked the driver—a tall, round-shouldered, rugged old man dressed in damp tweeds and leather—if he were from Alata. He nodded and I got into the front seat—"for company" as I innocently said. There I remained alone for almost half an hour, until at last the driver joined me, muttering bitterly to himself something about "twa days running and now it will be a third." We drove off, he banging in the gears with the action, and expression, of a boxer making a short-arm jab. I had enough to think about and left him to himself.

But soon we were in glens so wild and lovely that I had that very human desire to talk and share. I asked: "Who does this land belong to?"

"Prince Charlie," he answered in a tone of angry surprise —and that was the extent of our conversation.

After about an hour we came over a pass and had a view of the western Ocean. It was evening by now and half the sky was lighting up in a vast diorama of pastel shades which were reflected in the sea. We lost most of this as we zig-zagged down into the valley, but I felt sure we must see it again. We did, ten minutes later, when the road reached the coast. By then the colors were much stronger, like flames and blood. And on a promontory with cliffs, outlined against this background, was a castle—not a large one but a real old castle built for defence. We swept through a black firwood, through a gate and into a drive lined by enormous rhodo-dendrons. The driver put the car into neutral and we coasted down to the grim old building by the shore.

We drew up outside the granite entrance. The driver carried my bag into the hall. This was large, brightly lighted and expensively furnished, but in a way which would have better suited an up-to-date club than an ancient castle. It was a shock to say the least, coming in from the bleak and genuine exterior.

"They'll be in the turret room," the driver said.

He slid a panel and we were in an elevator, all chromium plate and mirrors. He pressed the top button and we shot upwards.

We stepped out into a small carpeted antechamber where there was only the head of a spiral staircase and a single door. This the driver opened and said loudly: "Here he is. Just the one."

I was in a large, oak-paneled, comfortably furnished room with bay windows which looked out onto the sea and the sunset. There were big leather armchairs and a refectory table with bottles and glasses on it.

Two men jumped up as I came in. One was Natham. The other was a leaner, more rangy figure who after the first quick movement stood with his hands in his pockets and his chin on his chest. But I could not see him clearly then because the lights had not yet been switched on.

"Are you alone?" Natham asked.

"Yes," I answered.

He went quickly past me to the door and shouted:

"Callum! Callum! Why—?"

The driver's angry voice came back.

"She was not on board."

"Are you quite sure?"

"Sure as I can be when ye don't tell me your visitor's names. Mr. Jonathan, of all the daft—"

Natham closed the door and came back into the room. He was clearly upset, but he controlled himself.

"Introductions," he said. "We have decided— I hope you

will not think it exaggerated—to stick to nicknames. What will you be?"

"Anything you like," I answered. "What about Scribe? I hope that is to be my job."

"Very good, Scribe. This is Biscuit. I am Bulldog. Most unfortunately, as you must have realized, Sea-Wyf has not come."

CHAPTER SEVEN

"MORE venison?" Bulldog asked. "Please do. You must be hungry." He carved it and handed me the plate.

"As I was saying," he went on, "my Uncle Herbert modernized the castle—quite ruthlessly as you see. For him the phrase good taste only applied to food. Ha-ha!" Bulldog looked at his two guests, evidently expecting applause. "You should see the kitchen—full of electric gadgets. But the whole castle is like that. One must not grumble—at least it enables Callum and his wife to run the place alone."

"Are they really the only servants you have?" Biscuit asked.

Our host laughed again. "You still think there must be others hidden away somewhere after twenty-four hours in the place. Alas no. They all walked out on me three weeks ago just because I prosecuted a laundry maid for stealing linen. They are as clannish as they can be. Everybody is related. So I could not get local replacements. Nor can I get outside girls, not with the nearest cinema forty miles away."

"What about Callum and his wife?" Biscuit asked.

"They came with me from the mainland. He has been with my family since I was a child. That is why he feels privileged and is so abominably rude . . . . But I am not looking after

61

you. Please help yourself to some more wine. By the way, you must remind me to show you the cellar. In Jacobite days it was used for storing the clan's forbidden weapons. Plenty of room. My uncle stocked it with loving care and, I think, with knowledge."

"Indeed he did. This is excellent claret," Biscuit said. "But Jacobite cellars! Is the castle haunted?"

"If it once was, Uncle Herbert exorcised it. Did you ever hear of a phantom coming up in an elevator? If there remains any ghost to lay it is a modern one."

Callum came in to clear and tidy, and put a decanter of port on the table.

"Is there anything else ye'll be wanting, Mr. Jonathan?" he asked.

"I will ring if there is," Bulldog said.

"Ring! Oh aye—and if they cut the current again would ye have an old man climbing those black stairs? Can ye no tell—?"

"Put out another bottle of whisky."

"There's plenty already. Mr. Jonathan—"

"Do as I say."

I turned away and began a conversation with Biscuit. He interested me. If I had to compare him to anything I would say he was like a monkey. But I could not blame Henry for not telling me he had simian features because he had not. The similarity, if one could generalize at all, was with a boy's face, round and smooth—although wrinkled about the eyes —and snubnosed. It was the eyes that had the monkey look—

sad and knowing together—and perhaps the loose-limbed way of moving, of stretching out an arm to pick up a wine glass as if he were going to pick a chestnut out of the fire. I did not entirely like Biscuit but he attracted me. I suspected that he had a sense of humor which was more than Bulldog had.

"Shall we move to the armchairs?" Bulldog said. "Would you like a brandy or a whisky and soda?"

We settled ourselves comfortably. I lit a pipe, Biscuit a cigarette, Bulldog a cigar. We smoked in silence with the murmur of the sea coming from below through the open window.

"Scribe," Bulldog said. "There is plenty of writing paper in that cupboard."

"Oh yes."

"I suggest you take down everything in shorthand notes. Afterwards you can speak it into a dictaphone or type it out yourself, just as you prefer. Then if necessary it could be published within two or three days."

I sat up.

"I'm prepared to work as hard as you like, but I'm afraid books aren't written and published as quickly as that."

"I know, I know," Bulldog said, looking at the ash of his cigar. "But the first essential is to prepare a factual account which we are all three prepared to sign. If we decide to publish it will have to be done at the very shortest notice. You have worked for a newspaper, I believe."

"Yes," I said.

"Excellent. Then you know how to handle such things. As you rightly say, a book would take too long. If we publish it will have to be in a newspaper. Biscuit tells me that in reply to his advertisement for a publisher he received a wire from the editor of a Sunday newspaper. We might make conditional arrangements with that paper."

"Have you started any negotiations?" I asked.

"No. There must be no risk of anything except the whole, agreed story being published. Therefore the typescript is the first essential."

Bulldog took a drink, then continued speaking in his rapid, precise way.

"I got in touch with Biscuit through his Box Number. I explained the circumstances—which we will deal with later —saying that I felt we were justified in breaking our compact and meeting in this quiet place to consult. He came at once. Upon his arrival I told him that I had also invited not only Sea-Wyf but yourself. After some discussion he saw my point. We need a text to which we all agree. That alone could counter any—any other version. Such a text must be prepared by an impartial outsider, but preferably one who already knows something about the story and is sufficiently interested in it to work hard. That is why I took you at your word and invited you here so—I am afraid—peremptorily. We are both most grateful to you for coming. Unfortunately Sea-Wyf has not answered my appeal. I wrote to her care of the *Daily Telegraph*, thinking she would certainly have given her true address when she sent in her announcements. But,

all I can say is: she is not here. We must start without her.
We will begin with the voyage in the ship. I will speak while
Biscuit corrects or supplements—then the other way round.
Are you ready, Scribe?"

"May I ask some questions before you begin?" I said.

"If you wish," Bulldog answered. "But any point of
which you may be in doubt will almost certainly be cleared
up in the ordinary course of the narrative."

I have decided not to give the story here in the form that
it was told to me, with the two men interrupting each other
and often arguing for minutes together on some seemingly
trivial point. Nor will I give the condensed statement which
Bulldog intended. Instead I shall repeat fully everything per-
tinent which was told me both then and later, in as straightforward a manner as I can and drawing the characters as I
came to see them. I believe it to be as accurate an account as
it is possible to give.

The *San Felix* was a merchant vessel of some two thous-
and tons which picked up her cargoes where she could, a
free lance of the five oceans. The Captain was a Greek, his
officers Europeans or Americans, and his crew, lascars. The
vessel sailed under the flag of Panama. In January, 1942, she
was in Singapore. With the Japanese at the gates, most of
the inhabitants of that cosmopolitan town were most anx-

ious to get away—almost anywhere so long as it was far away.

The Captain loaded the ship with refugees whom he undertook to transport to Mombasa where he hoped to pick up a conventional cargo from an agent with whom he dealt. He had cabin accommodation for five passengers. This he sold to fifteen men and women. In addition, the whole cargo space—decks and holds—was given over to evacuees—planters and officials from the interior, some with their wives and families, missionaries, civil servants, businessmen of various nations; and there were besides a large number of Chinese, chiefly of the shopkeeper sort, who preferred emigration at any price to waiting for the Japanese. No one except presumably the Captain and the purser knew the total number of passengers, but it must have exceeded a thousand.

The night of embarkation was one of frightened crowds, confusion and uncertainty. There was an air raid in progress and a number of other ships were also loading. One of the two men who later became known to each other as Bulldog and Biscuit had managed to secure a cabin, the other only a deck passage. But both, when they saw the overcrowded state of the vessel, sincerely wished that they had waited on the chance of official evacuation. But there was no turning back in that human river. Men and women, carrying all they could transport of their worldly goods, were squeezing and thrusting up the gangway where the purser, aided by a squad of sailors shepherded them to the quarters which they had been allotted.

As soon as the ship was fully loaded she cast off. The passengers in the blacked-out saloon studied each other and began the first skirmishes of conversation, behaving as much as possible as in peacetime voyaging. There was an American woman journalist, who did most of the talking. There was a pretty English lady, a Dutch couple and their daughter, a Frenchman with a wife who at first sight appeared to be almost entirely dressed in jewels. There were two elderly English spinsters, three rich Chinese, and three single European males—a clergyman, an advocate and an engineer.

The deck passengers had not this opportunity of examining each other. They were too preoccupied over keeping their possessions together and maintaining their stake of the deck, and they were not permitted any lights.

The ship's company was the link between the two classes of passengers. Of the Captain, a little man, nothing had yet been seen except his grizzled head above the bridge rail. The first officer spoke like an American. He was freckled and companionable. The purser was the busiest man on board during the first twenty-four hours. He was a mulatto, dark-skinned and crinkly haired, a fine fellow with an enormous chest, but he was a cripple in one leg. He used crutch sticks, the sort which are gripped with the hands and have an extension upwards to bracket the forearm. His approach could be recognized even in the darkness because although the rubber-ended sticks were silent his shoe made a noise like someone walking with a very slow and heavy-footed stride. The first engineer was a Scot.

The story had gone as far as this when the lights went out. Bulldog became very angry indeed. He groped in the dark for candles—and as soon as he had found them the electricity came on again, which made him angrier still. The thread of the story was broken, although a side light had been thrown on one of the characters. I took the opportunity to excuse myself, for after nearly twenty-four hours of travel I was too sleepy to make intelligible notes.

Bulldog took me to my room on the floor below, and I got into a comfortable bed. For a little while I lay in the darkness thinking of the events of the day. It was evident that my holiday, as a holiday, had ceased to exist. I would have to have a good rest at the office when I got back.

I smiled for there is a special pleasure in making a joke to oneself. But soon I was serious again, and in the way which sometimes happens when one is highly strung and very tired I became afraid. I felt that I had become involved in something more serious than I had expected. I could hear the waves. The castle was a ship ploughing through a hostile ocean. She was overcrowded with human beings and I knew she would be sunk. My muscles became tense, waiting for the blow, the horrible explosion which suddenly would come.

CHAPTER EIGHT

I<small>T</small> was on January 31 that the *San Felix* sailed. There followed a couple of days of intense anxiety while she dodged among the islands off the east Sumatran coast and slipped in darkness through the Sunda Straits. But once she was well out into the Indian Ocean, and nothing more alarming had been sighted than a few distant aircraft, this state of tension began to ease. The passengers adjusted themselves to each other and to their surroundings.

A ship at sea is like a little world in space, particularly when radio silence has to be maintained. The *San Felix* was a desperately overcrowded world, and since even her decks were made of iron she became hot as an oven under the tropical sun. The cabin passengers, though they were three to each small cabin and had no more room than anybody else in which to walk about, at least enjoyed the comparative comfort of the saloon where there was a bar and padded seats and —best of all—an electric fan.

Naturally they offered to share these amenities with those of the deck passengers who excited their pity. But this the Captain sternly forbade. If an invasion from the deck once started, he said, it would be impossible to know where it would end. The Asiatics would not be slow to take advantage. The two classes must remain strictly segregated.

The fifteen privileged people in the saloon quickly developed personalities, all more or less surprising. The loud-tongued lady journalist, who had at first appeared as hard and egocentric as a nail, joined forces with the mild English spinsters in defiance of the Captain's edict. With one or two of their male companions whom they had pressed into service they made what they described as forays into the jungle —and it was something like that, wading through the human forest—carrying refreshments, books and magazines.

The ship's officers ate with the cabin passengers, which helps to explain why the Captain insisted upon reserving these quarters. But at meals the ladies used to talk in stage whispers about what they had done and seen. There was an unfortunate man with two broken ribs, they said. Some women from a mission had been in the middle of a whole dump of Chinese, but they had persuaded the first officer to let them use a small deck house where they could be decently private. The people in the bow had to go fifty yards, stepping over or onto bodies in the dark to reach the lavatory. The lascar crew did nothing about keeping the decks clean. They were an undisciplined lot, and the officers seemed content to let them behave just as they pleased.

The Captain, whether or not he heard and understood what was being said, went on with his dinner. And his officers took the cue from him and were equally unresponsive. But this did not improve the atmosphere in the saloon. The *San Felix* was not a happy ship.

When the officers were absent on their duties their ears must have tingled. Criticism of them was the main subject of conversation. The Captain was an unprincipled ruffian. Even the cheerful, companionable first officer was disliked as a hypocrite. As for the mulatto purser, he could do nothing right. (That, actually, was almost correct, for although he worked indefatigably his job of pleasing everybody was impossible). At first some of the ladies had referred to him as "the poor purser," but when the effects of overcrowding became more and more apparent, he was held responsible. Also it was said that he favored the Asiatics at the expense of the whites. When approached with any complaint he always answered politely, even servilely. But he had one small and tiresome habit which, disproportionately, annoyed people most of all. Whenever he sat down, in his office or in the saloon, he somehow managed to place his sticks in a way that somebody was bound to trip over them. Then he would apologize profusely, hopping up and bowing his crinkled-haired head—but the same thing would happen again.

The only saloon passengers who did not join in these petty criticisms were the advocate, the three Chinese who rarely came out of their cabin and the sad young English lady who, it transpired, had just lost her husband.

The advocate, who was accepted as the leader, concentrated upon more important things. He approached the Captain with a strong plea for the institution of boat drill. But for the first time in his career he was completely at a loss when the little Greek answered blandly that there were only boats enough for one in ten and drill by itself never saved anybody.

The deck passengers were too many and too varied to elect a leader. They had their grievances, but on the whole they were philosophical about them. They had settled down to a camping life which, according to their natures and nationalities, was either of resigned squalor or ingenious improvisation. There were so many of them that they could only converse with those who directly surrounded them. A few chanted complaints to the officers as they went about the deck, and there were quarrels with the lascar crew. Generally, however, they were patient and well-behaved. The only disturbing factor was that in spite of the standing orders for silence after dark there were often wild bursts of singing, which suggested that there was a good deal of alcohol on board.

The *San Felix* chugged along at seven or eight knots. Naturally she did not keep to a shipping lane, nor did the Captain disclose the course that he was following. All that the passengers knew was that they were traveling roughly westwards through a vast and apparently empty ocean. And, after a week, that they must be beyond bombing range. It was merely a matter of putting up with things for perhaps another fortnight.

It was on February 15, the day when Singapore fell, that the ship was sunk. At 11 P.M. the women cabin passengers had retired to bed. In the saloon there were only the advocate and the Dutchman who were playing chess and two other men who were talking over drinks with the first officer. On deck all there was to be seen was a dim pattern of bodies lying close together. There was the soft murmur of a few voices and even sounds of sleep—that and the continuous swish-swish of the bow wave, for it was a calm night. It would be difficult to imagine a more peaceful scene than that which existed when six bells were sounded.

A few moments later the saloon was in complete disorder, tables and chairs smashed and scattered and the men sprawled anyhow. In that stunned interval before those who had not been killed came violently to life, the ship's cat streaked through the desolation with its tail straight out behind.

Then the din started—screams, the shouting of names, the shouting of orders, groans, wailings, and the noise of machinery breaking up. The ship looked as if she had stuck her nose into mud. In fact her bow had been blown off and her stern was rising as she sank. Those who could move on deck were trying to struggle aft up the increasing slope. Those who could not move were being slid and rolled towards the bow as a dump truck unloads gravel. Orders were being bellowed from the bridge. Officers and sailors were trying to obey them. Everyone with life in him was trying to do something, doing it earnestly, desperately—though it might be the most absurd thing to do. Men were plunging and scrambling about the deck, wild-eyed, endlessly calling out the name of somebody who did not answer. A native woman was trying to gather in her arms a score of little packages. Every time she picked them up they were sent flying and she would begin again to gather them. A good many of those who had secured life belts were stripping off their clothes and jumping over the side. Others crouched praying. There was an attempt at singing, Nearer My God to Thee. It was drowned in frantic curses.

The *San Felix* carried two lifeboats about thirty feet in length, one on each side of the deck. She also carried two much smaller craft which were slung to port and starboard of the bridge. Both of these latter and one of the larger boats were launched. But one of the small craft was holed and destroyed by men jumping into her from the deck. The large boat, which had been filled mainly with women and children, capsized and spilled everybody into the water.

About the second small boat, which was the last to be launched, there was a wild rush of men. Three revolver shots rang out and the rush ceased. But the boat went down with a run, the ropes screaming over the tackles. She slapped into the water and drifted away with scarcely anybody in her.

By now the stern of the vessel was sticking up at a crazy angle. It was impossible to remain on the deck without clinging onto something, but a number of people did remain on it. One woman was sitting astride the base of a ventilator feverishly going through her handbag. A number of Chinese were clinging to projections with both arms and legs, as incapable of moving as people become from vertigo on a mountain face. Others climbed towards the high stern.

But most of the ship's complement were in the water—swimming, drowning, holding to wreckage, or if they were lucky scrambling into a boat. The din continued undiminished: appeals for help, an occasional shout of encouragement, wailings and gurgling sounds, and above it all a high-pitched whistle of steam from the mortally wounded vessel.

She seemed to remain standing on her bow for a long time, a black pillar in the opal night. Now and then someone or something would fall from her and splash into the sea. On the stern rail, the highest point, the cat remained balancing. Its form could be distinguished against the light of the low moon. And all around on the still water was a debris of human beings and wreckage. But men and women who had to struggle for their lives still watched the ship, could not take their eyes from her.

Then the still water begun to boil. It bubbled up in mounds which spilled over, it seethed and heaved. The ship was going down rapidly. There was an explosion of steam as the engine went under. Within seconds the *San Felix* had disappeared completely. A vast quantity of water poured downwards with her, later to come rushing up again. Concentric waves raced outwards, fighting with the leisurely ocean swell, rocking the debris, tossing it about, making it spin. There was almost silence for a little while. But the shouting soon began again.

The moon went down into the sea and it was very dark. The shouts for help became spasmodic. Voice after voice was drowned. (One could hear them drowning). There were other sounds—the splash of oars or of swimming, dull or violent noises, shrill cries of pain, despair, misery.

The dark night seemed interminable and full of terror. "Sharks!" a voice screamed. "Sharks! Sharks! Sharks!" And another wave of panic swept like a pestilence of madness through those who were still alive.

CHAPTER NINE

THE sun came up and the enormous piles of cloud which had looked black against the paling sky of dawn were suddenly ignited. They blazed, writhing while they did so as burning paper writhes. They burned themselves out into white masses like powdery ash which still heaved and swelled and contracted against the hardening blue of the sky . . . . But although the clouds seemed to have cooled, the rest of the world became hotter every minute.

On the oily swell the debris still remained. It was widely dispersed—it covered a square mile or more—but it was still upon the scene of the wreck.

It consisted of packing cases, broken spars and furniture, a sun helmet, life belts, bottles, straw mattresses, oranges and kitchen refuse, hairbrushes, buckets and brooms, planks from a smashed boat and a large quantity of unrecognizable pieces of wood such as the landsman finds washed up upon the shore. To some of the larger fragments men were still clinging, for the warm sea was cruel in that it killed very slowly those who had the courage to hold on. There were besides two craft, the large lifeboat and one of the small ones. These were tightly packed with human beings and were lying about a hundred yards apart. A good quarter of a mile from both craft and on the outskirts of the littered area was a small emergency float. A number of such rubber floats had been lashed to the deck of the *San Felix* but all the rest had gone down with her because in the confusion nobody had thought of cutting them free and inflating them. There were two men on this float. When they first became visible at dawn they were paddling away northwards, but as soon as the sun grew hot they gave up this exertion and allowed their tiny craft to drift.

The two boats were so crowded that only those who were against the gunwales and faced outwards could even move their arms. The men in this favorable position were almost all lascars of the crew. Those who stood crowded together inboard, pressed as tightly together as sticks of asparagus in a bunch, and already drooping with exhaustion, were men and a few women of half a dozen different nationalities with a preponderance of Chinese. Apart from the purser and the third engineer, there were none of the officers on either of the boats. These may have gone down with the ship. But some at least had died even more violent deaths. When the boats were full, no one else had been allowed even to hold onto the gunwale, let alone scramble on board. Oars were used for other purposes than rowing. Terrible things were done in the frantic passion of self-preservation. Besides, the

San Felix had never been a happy ship and undoubtedly there were secret grudges to be paid off.

The coming of daylight was welcomed by the survivors—but not for long. Although the darkness had been terrifying at least it had been cool and had concealed some of the things which happened among those leaderless and fatally mixed crowds. In daylight the rapid breakdown of morale could be observed in detail.

The two main hardships which persisted were the crowding and the heat. As has been said there was no room to move. Men and women, all more or less naked, were literally pressed against each other. They had been like that during perhaps five hours of darkness and now they had ten or twelve of sunshine to endure—with what hope after that? Each man was his fellow's enemy until there should be room to row or sail. And the heat made them physically revolting to one another. Besides there was no wind. The boats did not move. They remained quite still, and this increased the sense of being shut in. Yet they were not constricted by walls. All around them was an infinite amount of space. The temptation, the urge, was to get away, to be free of this sticky, suffocating mass of humanity at any cost.

During that morning a number of survivors lost the balance of their minds. The heavy silence was broken by a gaily idiotic shout, "Look, there's a fruit barrow. Come and buy some." There was a swaying in the crowd followed by a splash.

Sometimes it happened quite differently, a burst of furious

curses and the sound of blows. Or someone slipped away without a word, or suddenly exploded into action and dragged another with him. But the end was the same—a splash. It was difficult to see exactly what happened, but nobody much cared in any case.

Only two things stirred them. The first was the coming of the sharks. The panic shout just after the *San Felix* went down had apparently been a false alarm, or perhaps only one or two of the beasts had appeared. But a whole squadron of sharks arrived about noon. The black fins came slitting through the silky surface like the points of sharp knives thrust up from beneath. Fortunately most of those in the water had let go and disappeared before then. But there was one man who all morning had been within about thirty yards of the smaller boat, floating with his arms over a spar as a yokel leans upon a gate. From exhaustion or apathy he had not tried to reach the boat, but had remained with his eyes on it and his expression blank.

Suddenly this half dead face was contorted by a paroxysm of terror—and he vanished. There was a violent commotion, a lashing of great tails and the gleam of white bellies.

It did not take the sharks long to clean up. They were about the boats for only an hour. Then, as if on an order, they all went off. It had been like an organized raid.

The second incident which temporarily woke people from their self-centered misery occurred in the larger boat. A group of Asiatics near the bow who had for some time been whispering together, suddenly fell upon their knees and began stabbing and banging at the floor boards with row-locks and a sheath knife. They were put overboard before they could do any serious harm.

Such incident galvanized the survivors for a moment or two into some sort of common purpose. Then would have been a time for a strong man to assert himself as commander and create some sort of order and discipline. But no one could or would. They had been warned by incidents during the night. Anyone who interfered with what his half-crazed neighbor wanted to do almost inevitably involved himself in a fight, and those who fought were pushed out indiscriminately.

So, as the sun descended painfully slowly towards the western horizon, the last of the small ration of water in the boats was drunk by a few, or spilled. A case of preserved milk was broached, the tins punctured and handed round. A few asked, "How much are we supposed to drink?" But most went on sucking at the thick liquid until they either emptied the tin or had it snatched way from them. The biscuits were not all consumed only because it was impossible to eat them dry. A few tried soaking them in sea water. Others attempted to hoard them in their pockets, if they had clothes. The stores were scanty in any case for the boats had been stocked for a fraction of the numbers which were aboard them. And from the smaller boat a tin of meat was lost by a man snatching it up in his arms and jumping overboard. Like those who had tried to hole the boat, men who had lost the will to live wanted to destroy.

At best, they thought no further than the present. The sails were torn up to make hats and shoulder coverings against the sun. It was suicide. Everyone who still had his wits about him knew that, yet could do nothing to prevent it.

Sunset, longed for in the torturing heat of noon, became a thing to fear as it approached—because it would bring darkness. And to accentuate this feeling came one more incident, far removed yet disturbing.

All day the little float had been lying on the water. The two men aboard it had remained sitting down, apparently doing nothing. They had been vaguely envied just because they could sit down, or move if they wished. If anyone in the boats had thought of trying to join them, the sharks had changed his mind. But the float was something to look at in the waste of sea. Occasionally one of the watchers had yelled out crazily that it was an island or a rescue ship. But for the sane it had remained something definite, removed from the madness which they feared.

And then the two men aboard it jumped to their feet and began to wrestle. For several minutes they swayed and turned as if engaged in a crazy dance. The float tilted at all angles as they heaved about. At last, still locked together, they went overboard. The inhabitants of that tiny world who had appeared so fortunate had destroyed themselves.

For an hour or two nothing else happened at all. Sunset was blazing in the sky when a woman went over the side of the larger float. This sort of thing had became so usual that her companions scarcely turned their heads. But there was a difference here. When others had splashed into the water they had disappeared at once or very soon. They had not even tried to keep upon the surface. But she struck out strongly in a calm and steady breast stroke. And soon it was apparent that she was swimming towards the float. She would be drowned or taken by a shark, no doubt. But she was watched as something to look at. Bloodshot eyes moved listlessly, searching the endless water for an approaching fin.

Man's fear of sharks is deeper and more sickening than that of snakes. It belongs to an element in which he is comparatively helpless, and sharks kill so revoltingly. Yet fear like discomfort is comparative. Could sharks be worse than the inevitability of another night in the boats, with other days and nights to follow, and no hope? Someone had shown an alternative.

A man plunged from the same boat and struck out after the woman. He was not a good swimmer, his arms splashed clumsily, but he kept going with determination. Then from the other boat a second man dived in and, also clumsily, began to converge upon the other swimmers, making for the float.

All three, two a hundred yards in front and the other following, were a long time in the water. They went slower and slower. Often they changed their strokes or rested on their backs. But they kept going somehow. The first man caught up with the woman. They struggled on side by side, just moving. A few minutes before the sun set the leading pair reached the float and after a good deal of kicking and splashing managed to slither on board. The second man got within twenty yards of the float and then his slowly moving head went under water.

The watchers on the two boats turned away, once more wrapped in their own destinies.

CHAPTER TEN

WHEN the woman and the first man had succeeded in wriggling onto the float they were at first too exhausted to do anything but lie still. Then the man sat up, and the woman with a sudden movement rolled away from him. The float tilted dangerously.

"Steady. I won't hurt you," he said. His voice was a harsh whisper. "Are you English?"

She was watching him intently, head down and shoulders rounded, her hands gathering together what remained of a nightdress. It was already dusk and they could not see each other clearly. She nodded but did not speak. He turned away from her troubled stare.

The next moment the float rocked again as he scrambled up, reaching for an earthware demijohn, its handle secured by a length of cord to the side of the float. He grabbed it up and there was a murmur of liquid inside it. "God! half full." He unscrewed the stopper, lifted the big flask nearly to his lips, then suddenly thrust it out towards the woman.

Slowly, with the doubtful movements of a sleepwalker, her hands took it. But it was so heavy that he had to support it, and he tilted it too much. She choked, rubbed the spilled liquid violently from her face, and shook her head.

"All right, don't." He put it to his own lips. After the first mouthful he checked and blew out his breath, then took a drink. While he was still drinking his foot kicked a biscuit tin which was on the bottom of the float, and it clattered over, empty.

"Look," the woman said, speaking for the first time, in a tone of anxiety.

The man put down the demijohn and looked where she was pointing, at a second man who, twenty yards away, was splashing like a drowning dog, his head disappearing for a moment every now and then. The man on the float said nothing at first, but took another drink and slowly replaced the stopper, watching the swimmer sinking and coming up again. He laughed.

"Come on, you'll do it. That's the spirit!"

He laughed again.

The woman got upon her knees and, picking up a paddle from the bottom, tried to move the float towards the failing man. But it only spun round upon itself. This made the man beside her laugh still more. The swimmer had gone under altogether.

There was a second paddle in the float. She handed this to him with one word: "Help." Still chuckling he obeyed. A few seconds later the swimmer came to the surface again. The woman took a handful of his hair and supported him till he could grasp the rope which hung in loops round the side of the float. He rested for some time. At last he heaved himself up a little and with the others' assistance scrambled aboard. He lay gasping in the bottom.

"You're a bloody bulldog," the first man said. "But you might as well have drowned. We'll all be dead in the morning. Have this first."

He unscrewed the stopper of the demijohn.

Slowly and quite gently the woman took it from him. She laid it horizontally on one of the air tubes which formed the sides of the oval float. She tipped up the end of the demijohn. The liquid began to splash overboard.

The first man made a movement to stop her, then dropped his arms. He crouched watching, his mouth open, while the liquid continued to plop-plop-plop into the sea.

"Water," gasped the man who had been called a bloody bulldog.

"Gin," said the other man. "But it would have made dying more amusing. No water and no biscuit. Never mind, you can eat me if you really want to live"—his voice became hysterical. "Suck the blood, that is the thing to do. But you have to do it while the patient is still alive, otherwise it doesn't flow. Suppose this sounds revolting to you now, but in a few days—no, in less—"

"This will do nicely for holding water when it rains," the woman said in a matter-of-fact voice. She was quietly replacing the stopper of the demijohn. "It and the biscuit tin will hold a lot."

The man who was nearly mad checked himself and stared at her.

"Will it rain?" he asked like a child.

"Of course it will. Look at those clouds."

"Look at that!" The second man was sitting up. "A shark. Keep still."

"Coming straight at us," the other man whispered.

The brief dusk was turning into night. It had already swallowed the distant boats. But ploughing steadily through the smooth water was a phosphorescent line. They all three stared silently. It was not exactly a line for it faded out behind into the dark silk of the sea. But the front part glowed and burned with a million tiny particles of fire, and it advanced rapidly towards them.

"It's not a shark," the first man said.

"It is a man," said the woman.

"It can't be. It's coming too fast," the first man said. But they knew she was right, for they could make out the arms now, working rhythmically in a crawl stroke. The face was hidden, only breaking the surface to breathe.

"There is no room," the men of the float said together.

The swimmer paused for a moment to get his bearings, then came on with a final burst of speed. He grasped the side of the float and the phosphorescence streamed from his wide shoulders.

"You let me come on board?"

The three above him saw the flash of teeth as he spoke, the

appealing, humble eyes, the iris dark but ringed by gleaming white.

The woman, kneeling, held out both hands to him.

"Very kind," he said, taking her hands.

With the powerful undulation of a jumping salmon he came over the side and curled up his large body in the constricted space of the floor boards.

It was then they saw that he only had one leg.

None of them spoke much that night. When they did—too tired and far removed from ordinary life to introduce themselves—they found themselves using nicknames, words associated with their instinctive reactions to one another. They were Biscuit, Sea-Wyf, Bulldog and Number Four—though none of them could say afterwards exactly why they used these words. Presumably Number Four, as purser of the *San Felix*, knew their real names. But if so, he never spoke them.

As, consciously or unconsciously, they tried to escape from their real selves, so they did their best to get away from the scene of the disaster. During most of the night they took turns to paddle. In the best circumstances this would not have been easy. Worn out as they were, it was a terrible ordeal. The float was lozenge-shaped, its buoyancy and most of its rigidity depending on the inflated tubes which formed the sides. This made it awkward to use a paddle efficiently when sitting on the lasts of wood which covered the float bottom. So Biscuit and Bulldog knelt on one knee or the other. But they very soon became cramped, while the pain in the knee itself was not a thing to be borne for long. Sea-Wyf, who took her turn as a matter of course, was either more supple or more stoical about this, but her arms were weak. Much the most efficient paddler was Number Four. He squatted—to use the Biscuit expression—"cross-legged except that he only had one," and his back was long enough to enable him to use the paddle to good effect.

There had been some discussion on the course they ought to steer.

"Do you know where we were?" Bulldog asked Number Four. "No, you wouldn't. You weren't concerned with that side of things."

Number Four said nothing.

"Well I reckon from the time we were sailing we must be about two thousand miles west of Sumatra. That's just about the middle of the ocean, I suppose."

Biscuit nodded.

"No good trying to go back," Bulldog went on in a slow, painful croak, "no good going south—"

"No bloody good going west, if there's still two thousand miles to Africa," Biscuit said.

"Then north—"

"We must be south of the Equator. If you feel like crossing the Equator, I don't. Not much point going anywhere for that matter."

"There is! Apart from getting somewhere we don't want an invasion from the boats."

SEA≠WYF

The argument had been settled by a slight breeze which began to blow from the southeast, as well as they could judge. They went with it, north-westward.

The two who were not paddling reclined in the bow and stern, the paddlers being side by side amidships. They changed places with the utmost care. With the wind and their own exertions the water had begun to whisper and lap against the float. This gave an impression of speed. If one went overboard, one might be left behind. Besides, they did not quite trust each other for help in getting back on board. Only for a few minutes had they seen one another's faces, and that was hours ago. They had become dark shapes, bodies which it was almost impossible not to touch, unknowns, who might react with violence. All but one of them were of the same race, that was something. But the memory of the frenzied boats was still vivid. They had learned that human beings can be as dangerous as high explosive. They spoke and moved with care.

One of the voices rasped out suddenly, "Look, a ship!" On the water to the westward a bright light was burning. They all tried to shout but gave that up because it was so painful and no use. The light was evidently a long way off. So they remained silent and staring while the dawn light grew until the setting planet, which was what they were looking at, faded into the cruel blue of the sky.

They saw each other clearly then. Biscuit appeared to be in the worst condition of the four. He had long ago sobered from the neat alcohol he had drunk, but he showed its effect.

His face was haggard, his eyes deep sunk and ringed with shadow, and he was continually licking his dry lips. He was wearing only a pair of shorts. His lean body was hairy and muscular, but his limbs drooped.

Bulldog had on a shirt with one sleeve torn off and a pair of silk underpants. Dressed like that he could scarcely be an impressive figure. His unathletic legs were white as a fish's belly and his long face was red, puffy about the eyes. But his mouth was firm. He was evidently determined to go on living.

To begin with neither he nor Biscuit could take their eyes off Sea-Wyf. In spite of their exhaustion, their burning thirst, the hunger cramps in their stomachs, they were still men enough to wonder how on the *San Felix* they had failed to notice her. Even in her pitiable condition her face was lovely —youthful and bravely near serene. It was crowned by black hair cut short as a boy's, tousled and curly. Her skin was the color of honey. Her nose was small and straight, her mouth was rather wide. Although it was far from smiling one felt that it knew how to smile. But the most remarkable feature was the eyes. They were so dark that they seemed to be all pupil and therefore able to see and say far more than other eyes. . . . And there she sat curled up in the torn shift she wore, her remarkable eyes cast down.

The two Englishmen caught each other staring and both quickly turned away. They looked at Number Four. He did not meet their glance for he was still in manner the obsequious creature they had know on the *San Felix*. But clad only in trunks and sitting down he was like the statue of a Hercules cast in bronze. His arms and shoulders were particularly well developed, no doubt from walking with crutch sticks. So what had made him a pitiable cripple in that other world had strengthened the upper half of his body. Yet he was still grotesque. To move about he had to use his hands as a seal does its flippers.

He may have been embarrassed by this scrutiny. At any rate, murmuring something about a bath, he went over the side. For several minutes he swam about, his arms churning, his single leg flicking up and down and to each side with the action of a sculling oar. He played like a dolphin, he seemed to belong to the water.

At last he came on board again, undulating over the side with the momentum of his swimming. There he heaved himself awkwardly into his place in the stern, smiled apologetically and said that it was good to take a dip. You absorbed moisture through the skin. Did not the lady and gentlemen wish to bathe? He would keep watch for sharks.

None of them accepted.

CHAPTER ELEVEN

T<small>HE</small> three others did not bathe but made a sort of toilet by splashing their heads and faces and rinsing out their mouths. Biscuit even swallowed a few mouthfuls of sea water—although Bulldog told him he was a fool to do so—and said that he felt better for it. He looked refreshed.

After that, while the sun climbed higher in the sky and grew more hot, they sat for a while doing nothing, not even talk.

Sea-Wyf had not spoken since the evening before. She remained in the bow with averted eyes, looking troubled—not afraid, but troubled.

Bulldog and Biscuit glanced at her occasionally. But Number Four in the stern watched her continuously as if he were examining a picture. Seeing him doing this, Bulldog's face became even redder than before, and at last he burst out: "Can't you do anything else but stare, you unmannerly brute?"

Number Four's swarthy, round-eyed face became a picture of bewildered deprecation. He said that he had meant no offense. Later, he tried to start a conversation. But the two white men ignored him and at last he sank into an offended silence.

The strain was broken by Sea-Wyf asking what something was. At one end of the float, under the curve of the side tube, she had noticed a sort of pocket, its flap held down by a press stud. In it they found a triangular piece of red cotton which was evidently a sail. Only then did they realize that a thin six-foot spar lashed along the axis of the flooring, and which they had taken as an additional support, was in fact a mast. The lashings, unraveled, formed three guys. The mast-foot fitted into a notch in the floor boards.

This discovery spurred them to a more careful examination of their craft. They found another and smaller pocket which contained a concertina pump with a rubber tube ending in a nozzle which proved to fit into a valve on each of the lateral tubes of the float—an emergency means of inflation.

That was all they found, but it was enough to set the men talking while they stepped and guyed the mast.

"We'll push along much faster now," Bulldog said.

"Yes," said Biscuit, "we'll get nowhere in no time."

"What else can we do?"

"Do you remember when we were in those boats," Biscuit said slowly.

"Well?"

"I saw a floating orange."

"It would be uneatable."

"Then, yes. I'd had some tinned milk—hadn't you all? But now—my God!"

He passed a flannelly tongue over his lips, worked his throat muscles to form saliva, and went on.

"The sea was full of stuff. We ought to have hung about till morning. We might have salvaged any amount."

"And been swamped by others swimming from the boats."

They were silent for some time. It was impossible to talk without frequent rests to let the throat recover.

Biscuit asked: "How far do you suppose we came last night?"

They all looked back. The wide undulations of the swell were slightly corrugated by the breeze but otherwise the ocean looked exactly as it had the day before. On all sides it spread away and away and away to the circular horizon, and there was nothing on it at all to give an idea of scale. Distance did not have much meaning.

"Quite a long way." Bulldog said.

"I don't suppose we were doing more than one or two knots at most."

"We can't go back in any case, not against this wind," Bulldog said.

"We might hold our position here with the paddle and see if anything drifts past."

They tried to do this, but they could not tell if they were holding their position or not. Nor were they sure whether the same wind was blowing from exactly the same quarter as on the night before. It was certainly freshening, however, and Bulldog was impatient to set the sail.

"That would be crazy," Biscuit said.

"Why?"

"We can't possibly get anywhere. But if we hang around here there is a chance of rescue."

"Why? We are not on any shipping route."

"The radio man must have sent out an S O S."

"No. He scuttled like the rest."

"He might have. What do you think, Number Four?"

"I don't think nothing," Number Four answered, looking offended.

"Even if he did get one off and it was picked up, would another ship come to a place where a submarine was known to be?" Bulldog asked.

"It was a mine," Biscuit said.

"Whatever it was—"

Sea-Wyf raised her hand for silence. She was listening.

They all listened, searching the sky, shading their eyes with their hands. At last they saw the aircraft—a silver insect against the dazzling blue. They stood up and waved the red sail. They knew it was no use—the machine was too far off, but since there had been one airplane there might be more. Their hopes rose.

"If we had been where we were last evening we'd have had a chance," Biscuit said.

"It did not see the boats any more than us—"

"The lunatics must have scuppered them."

The argument continued until it dried up—literally.

Long before noon it became impossible to sit on anything except the wooden lasts of the flooring. The rubber had become so hot that it burned the skin, and it smelled sickeningly. They were still trying to paddle sufficiently to hold their position, but this became increasingly difficult to do.

"We are riding much higher," Bulldog said.

"Good God, of course!" It was almost a shout from Biscuit. "Look how they've swelled. They'll burst!"

The tubes had been gradually yet steadily inflating as the air inside them expanded in the heat. Now they were as tight as drums.

"We must let some out," Biscuit said. He put his hand to one of the metal valves and drew it back quickly, flicking his fingers.

"For Heaven's sake be careful," Bulldog said.

Biscuit splashed water over the valve until it was cool. Then, with an effort, he turned it. The air came screaming out.

The float rocked violently as both Biscuit and Bulldog tried to close the valve together. At last one of them succeeded, and they sat back on the floor boards, exhausted.

"I'll do the other," Bulldog said.

"No, I know how to do it now."

Biscuit handled the second valve more surely. But they were all relieved when the operation was finished.

"What about evening?" Bulldog asked. "When it gets cool."

"Then we must pump them up."

It was logic, but their craft seemed an even more fragile thing than it had before—frail as a bubble.

The heat became searing. It was impossible to paddle any more. They wet the sail and tried to hold it up as an awning. But at noon the area of shade was scarcely enough for one person. Besides, the sun shone through the thin cotton. The sun was cruel and cunning, searching them out and scorching them. They tried filling the biscuit tin over the side and pouring the water over their bodies. First Biscuit and then the other men took off their scant garments, damped them and put them on their heads. Sea-Wyf remained as she had all day, her eyes either downcast or staring out over the water.

"It is raining over there," she said at last.

Far away astern a dark cloud was moving over the sea, trailing what looked like a curtain of fine steel chains.

Rain! Fresh water. Cold water. They could not take their eyes off it. But it never came anywhere near them. Either from tact or weariness Biscuit did not repeat that they should have remained on the scene of the wreck—which was where they thought the rain had fallen. None of them said anything. Only their stomachs spoke now and then, loudly and angrily. But the hunger pains were nothing to the continuous nagging of thirst.

About midafternoon they saw another aircraft. Optimism soared up again—and with reason. For this machine was much lower than the last, and it did not fly straight. It swung up and down, evidently searching for something. It was visible for half an hour and once passed within only a few miles. Throughout this time the four people on the float waved and waved. But evidently they were not seen. The aircraft finally disappeared to the northward.

Painful though talking had become, they discussed this for some time. They were being searched for, not a doubt of it. Either an S O S had been picked up or else the first aircraft had reported seeing something on the water, and the Catalina—Bulldog said that the second aircraft was a Catalina —had been sent out.

Within a day or two they were certain to be found.

"But we have got to stay alive meanwhile. Pray God for rain," Bulldog concluded. "It's thirst that's killing us."

"I never thought of that," came Biscuit's rasping whisper.

Bulldog stared at him angrily.

"Fish," Biscuit said. "You pray for rain and I'll try to catch fish."

"How the devil?"

That was it. The life lines draped from the side tubes might make fishing lines but there was nothing whatever to use for either hooks or bait.

"I wonder if the sail might make a net," Biscuit said. "There are some little fish about. Look."

A school of minnows were swimming in the shade of the float. They seemed tame enough, but the red sail drove them away, and from fear of losing it Biscuit desisted. But he went on trying with the tin, now and then cooling the side tube with water so that he could lean over it.

Several times, by patient manipulation, he got a small fish into the tin. But every time he began to lift it the fish spilled out. At last he threw the tin into the bottom of the float, and gave up trying.

Towards evening the Catalina appeared again. But it was a long way off. They did not even wave to it. With increasing depression and lassitude they waited for the night.

The cool of evening revived them enough to undertake the alarming task of blowing up the tubes again. For some seconds they could not fit the pump nozzle properly into one of the valves and a good deal of air escaped with a shrill squeal which made them jump.

When at last the task was done, Biscuit said, "I'm glad that's over. It sounded like a pig being killed."

"Don't say that word!" Number Four almost shouted.

"What word?"

"That animal."

"A pig?"

"Don't say it. It's the worst bad luck to mention that animal at sea."

"Of all the damn fool superstitions!" Bulldog exclaimed.

By this time it was too late usefully to continue looking out for aircraft or for drifting stores and wreckage. There was nothing to do but compose themselves for the night.

They were dreading the night, in spite of the coolness. They sat in silence until one by one they dropped off into uneasy dreams.

They were awakened by the soft voice of Sea-Wyf.

"I hear something."

They listened. There was the lapping of water against the float. That was all Bulldog and Biscuit could hear. But when Number Four was appealed to by Sea-Wyf he agreed that there was something else.

"Where?"

He pointed up wind.

They all continued to listen intently. Although anything must surely be better than nothing in that waste of ocean they felt their slow pulses quickening with fear of the unknown.

"What is it?" Bulldog asked Number Four.

"I don't know nothing."

"What do you think, Sea-Wyf?"

"An engine."

Wild thoughts raced through their minds. The Catalina had spotted the boats and come down on the water. Or a launch had been sent out to rescue. Whatever it was they must get there. They picked up the paddles and drove their little craft along.

Now and then they stopped to listen. Quite soon they could all hear it clearly, the steady chug-chug-chug-chug-chug of some motor. It did not sound like an airplane, not quite like a ship. It remained in the same place. But it was real—that was all which mattered. In spite of their exhaustion they paddled on and on.

Then, when it must still have been a long way off, the sound ceased.

CHAPTER TWELVE

AFTER listening for some time and hearing nothing, Bulldog and Biscuit began to paddle again. They had to force themselves to make the effort. They felt that another day without water would kill them. They *had* to find help before the murderous sun came up.

They did not know the time. (They had no idea how to tell it by the stars.) They supposed it had been two or three hours after midnight when Sea-Wyf had heard the sound. Dawn might be near. At first they had taken turns to paddle. But that did not work any longer. The effort of changing places counteracted the effects of rest. The woman wanted to help but could not any more. Number Four, although he had looked in fairly good condition before sunset, had merely let his paddle drift through the water. Either he was still offended by the angry words of the morning on which he seemed to have been brooding since, or else he had resigned himself to die.

At any rate, Biscuit and Bulldog had to do the paddling. The pain they endured during the following hour or so was an example of what men can be driven to by the strongest of all instincts, the will to live. They were so tired that it hurt their necks to keep their heads upright, or to let them droop. Kneeling, a devil with red-hot fingers was playing scales upon their vertebrae. Their knees were rubbed, their thighs and calves frequently knotted by cramps, their hands blistered. And the fibers of their arm and shoulder muscles, which had to do most of the work, were splintering like broken wood. But they kept on.

They could only steer up wind. It would be easy to pass within a hundred yards of the boat—or whatever it was—without seeing it. That was the excuse for stopping frequently to listen. But they heard nothing except the gentle lapping of water on the float, and their own sawing breath. Number Four sat like a one-legged Buddha in the stern. Sea-Wyf in the bow was tense as a figurehead. And it was she who saw the thing—"

"There!"

The eastern sky had become a silvery gray. Looking where the girl pointed they saw a dark bulge on the water. It might have been a whale, but not quite. It was man-made. They tried to shout, which hurt their throats but produced practically no sound at all. Biscuit and Bulldog began paddling again, splashing out of time with each other, intoxicated with hope—with more than that, the certainty of rescue.

No voice came from the strange craft in front. But as they drew near they heard the sudden metallic click of a weapon being cocked. That stopped them paddling.

The next moment a blinding light shot out at them. It hurt their eyes so that they had to cover them. There was a whisper of voices. The light left them for perhaps ten seconds and swung round in a circle like a lighthouse beam. Then it pounced on them again and held them mercilessly while they cowered, naked and with their hands over their faces, as if praying.

The float drifted on and bumped gently against the submarine. By the feel, somebody grabbed the looped rope and made it fast. The brilliant light went out but another—much less strong, probably a flashlight—took its place. This played over them, keeping them blinded although it did not hurt as the searchlight had. There was a murmur of unintelligible voices and the sound of feet.

A voice rose, sharp and sudden, questioning. They did not understand. The question was repeated.

"English," Bulldog managed to say.

"Shipwrecked. Put that light out. Give us drink," Biscuit croaked.

Again there was a murmur of voices and the sound of footsteps. Meanwhile the light continued to play over them and the float, probing everything.

Then a new voice spoke from behind the light—high-pitched, staccato, on a single note.

"Who are you—English, American?"

"English," Bulldog answered, and the light was directed upon him.

"What are you doing?"

"We are on a pleasure cruise," Biscuit whispered.

The light switched onto him.

"What did you say?"

"Ship sunk night before last. No water or food."

"What did you say about pleasure?"

"Nothing. A joke—"

"What do you mean by a joke?"

After each question there was a murmur like an echo as the answer was interpreted. Then a different man spoke, putting the next questions to be translated by the high-pitched voice. The light still shone upon whoever replied, but it was less troublesome now because the daylight was growing fast.

"My friend is ill. No water—nothing—since—then," Bulldog managed to say.

"What was your ship?"

"*San Felix.*"

"Speak more loudly, please. From which port?"

"Sing—" Bulldog's voice broke and he bent his head, coughing silently.

"Give us water if you want answers," said Biscuit who had been working his throat muscles to lubricate them for this scarcely audible outburst.

"What did you say?"

Biscuit, who had the light on him, pointed at his dry tongue.

There was a pause, followed by what sounded like an order. A minute later a metal container was handed onto the float. Sea-Wyf drank first, then the others in turn. They had about a pint each. Feeling the liquid pouring into them was a sensation of exquisite pleasure—yet not satisfying. The water seemed to disappear into sand halfway down their throats. They wanted more. But when the container had gone round a second time it was empty. And they got no more, only questions.

What nationality was the *San Felix*? Her tonnage? How many passengers? Where were they now? Where had they been bound? What other ships had left Singapore at the same time, and where bound? What British and American warships were in the Indian Ocean? What bases were they using? Why had they thrown overboard their radio transmitter— the one with which they had signaled the Catalina?

Sea-Wyf and Number Four remained silent under this barrage of questions, put in English by the impersonal voice. Bulldog or Biscuit answered some of them. To the rest they were silent or said they did not know. The water had made it possible to speak but they were lightheaded with weariness and hunger. All this was such nonsense, such waste of time. In fact it could not have occupied more than five minutes, but it seemed interminable.

Meanwhile the sun broke surface and it was light. They saw the Commander of the submarine, a square man somehow patriarchal and out of place on a modern engine of war. He stood, head bowed and hands behind his back, aloof as in a shrine, not looking at them, listening only to the thin, spectacled interpreter by his side. Beside them on the deck of the submarine were four or five sailors with weapons at the ready. It was fantastic, this armed suspicion facing four almost naked castaways who were near the limits of exhaustion. It was hard to realize they were not dreaming.

"You refuse to tell any more?" the interpreter chanted without a hint of emotion.

"We do not know any more," Bulldog said wearily.

"The reason is immaterial. If you do not give information you are useless. You Westerners are finished before the rising sun of Japan—" he made a gesture towards the burning disk behind him— "We have serious duty to perform. My honorable Commander says Good-by."

An order was given and a sailor knelt down to cast loose the float.

"We need water and food," Biscuit said.

"My Commander regrets that he has nothing to spare. We are on special mission far from base."

"If you will not supply us, we are compelled to give ourselves up as your prisoners," Bulldog said.

There was a brief consultation. Then, "My Commander regrets that he has no space for prisoners. He does not shoot noncombatants, but if you are not prepared to die honorably by your own hands he is prepared as a humane man to slit your boat open with a sword."

There was a stunned silence.

"What you say he suggests is murder," Bulldog broke out. "It is against every code of civilized nations."

"On the contrary, my Commander is behaving strictly according to international law in leaving civilian unmolested. Besides—" The interpreter made a gesture which took in all the blankness of the ocean and the emptiness of the sky. The Commander himself did not even raise his heavy-lidded eyes. He had never looked at any of them at all.

Then Sea-Wyf spoke for the first time, quietly yet earnestly.

"Your Commander described himself as a humane man. I am sure he is. For the sake of common humanity I appeal to him, not to turn away from unfortunates, leaving them to die from want. Whatever his religion that would be a sin he must not place upon his conscience."

In her poor torn shift, her hands clasped, her dark eyes fearless but appealing, the girl waited for a reply.

When her words were translated to him, the Commander slightly shrugged his shoulders. He was looking at the sailor who was kneeling at his feet, still holding the trailing rope of the float. He opened his mouth to give an order, but was interrupted by Number Four.

Number Four spoke to him directly, not through the interpreter and in a language which he understood. The Commander raised his head. The others, watching, saw him looking at Number Four as if for the first time he had recognized that there was at least one human being in the float. As the speech went on he nodded once or twice. His sailors, who until then had kept their fingers on their triggers, lowered their weapons slightly. Their masklike faces came to life. Biscuit and Bulldog could understand nothing at all, but at least a word or two must have conveyed something to Sea-Wyf, for when Number Four pointed towards her saying something, she exclaimed: "No! No!" vehemently. She was not heeded. Number Four went on speaking while the Commander and his crew continued to listen attentively.

When Number Four at last came to an end the Commander remained for some moments longer in the same attitude of attention, interestedly examining the one-legged man and his three companions, particularly the woman.

Then he gave an order. The metal container, the empty demijohn and biscuit tin were taken from the float and carried below. They were brought on deck again and put into the float. A white sailor's smock and a small parcel wrapped in oilcloth were handed to Sea-Wyf.

Directly this had been done the float was cast adrift.

Biscuit came out of a trance of amazement.

"Where is the nearest land?" he shouted.

The interpreter spread his hands, "There is land all round," he answered.

"How long to reach it?"

The submarine was already under way. The interpreter now stood alone upon the patch of deck. With his spectacled face and thin, straight figure he was like a schoolteacher who by unkind magic was being carried away from his class before he had instructed them. His voice rose to the familiar note. But for the first time there was a hint of pedagogic feeling in it—it was the first time that he had spoken for himself.

"Empty your minds," he called across the water. "You must learn to eat time."

Within a few minutes the submarine was hull-down, then out of sight. The four on the float were once more alone in mid-ocean.

CHAPTER THIRTEEN

"THOSE were the devils who torpedoed us," Bulldog said.

Biscuit nodded. He was sitting on the edge of the float, legs apart and arms dangling between, staring in the direction where the submarine had disappeared.

"Yes, I suppose we were torpedoed, and by them. . . . . Yet one misses them," he said. " 'You must learn to eat time.' What else have we got?"

Everything except the smock, which Sea-Wyf had already put on, and the parcel which had proved to contain a book, was laid out on the floor boards. The metal container and the demijohn were full of water. The biscuit tin steamed with a concoction of beans and fish which presumably had been intended as part of the crew's breakfast. There was also a bag of hardtack. Altogether there were about four gallons of water and twenty-five pounds of food.

"What shall we fix on as a daily ration?" Biscuit asked.

"I'll work it out," Bulldog said. "We decided we might be two thousand miles from Africa. Say we average twenty miles a day. That means a hundred days. Four gallons is thirty-two pints. Just over a third of a pint of water a day for the four of us— a twelfth of a pint each."

The faces of the others grew increasingly solemn while this calculation was being made.

"A very small whisky," Biscuit murmured.

"And the food," Bulldog went on. "Twenty-five pounds—a quarter of a pound a day—one ounce each."

"We can't live on that," Biscuit said.

"What else?"

"Optimism is better than mathematics."

"Your jokes are apt to be ill timed. You might have got us into bad trouble with the Japanese if I hadn't said you were ill."

"All right, all right! But how do you suppose you are going to measure it out?"

Number Four interrupted. "I take charge of the stores and issue them," he said.

The two white men turned and stared at him. For a moment surprise was stronger than any other emotion. Number Four's one virtue had been that he seemed to know his place. But now. . . .

"Who the deuce asked your opinion?" Bulldog demanded.

"I did not give opinion, I said what I will do," Number Four answered calmly in his deep voice.

"What you would do?"

"Yes, with my food and water."

"*Your* food and water?"

"The Commander gave it to me because of what I told him. Therefore it is mine."

The amazement of Bulldog and Biscuit had rapidly changed to anger. That the creature who had done no paddling the night before should talk like this now was intolerable. Bulldog leaned forward to gather up the stores as a demonstration of who was in charge, meaning next to say whatever might be necessary to complete the lesson. But directly he moved, Number Four who had been squatting in his usual position in the stern rose an inch or two upon his single leg as if it were a spring.

"Touch nothing," he said.

Bulldog glanced at Biscuit who was opposite him amidships. Then they both turned on Number Four. The mulatto was in the pose of a sprinter at the start of a race. His spread fingers were pressing on the floor boards and the muscles stood out upon his arms and shoulders.... The two white men hesitated, each waiting for the other to act. Into Bulldog's mind came a picture of the two former occupants of the float wrestling together until they both went overboard.

"What did you say to the submarine Commander?" he asked coldly.

"I told him—"

The eyes of Number Four, hard and quickly moving, had been flicking between Bulldog and Biscuit, half left and right. Now they settled between the two men, on the bow of the float, and his face became doubtful. Instinctively glancing round, Biscuit saw Sea-Wyf looking at Number Four with an expression of desperate appeal.

It was gone in a moment, and she said quietly, "Would you all be satisfied if I took charge of the rations? I know what is necessary."

They agreed gladly. The strain broken, Bulldog and Biscuit

were particularly affable to each other while they set the sail. Now and then they made some quite friendly remark to Number Four. He responded with a grin. But often he smiled to himself for no apparent reason. Sometimes he glanced at Sea-Wyf with a questioning expression. But she was always looking in another direction.

The float went well under the triangle of red sail. It bustled over the water like a little fat duck breasting the waves. It would only go before the wind, but that was as good a direction as they knew—roughly north-eastward. And it seemed to go fast. This may have been an illusion due to the smallness of the craft and the close proximity to the water of those on board, but the sense of speed was stimulating and they talked a good deal.

Sea-Wyf gave them each as much of the bean stew as they could balance on two fingers. They made a joke of the smallness of the meal and at the system she had chosen, for she got least of all. But this she said was fair: each would be fed in proportion to his size. They were all doing their best to be amicable, but even that innocent remark made the two white men look with disapproval at the big milk-chocolate colored hands of Number Four. It was difficult to find a safe topic.

Inevitably they got back to the submarine. They agreed that it must have been compelled by the hunting Catalina to spend most of the previous day submerged, and had come up at night to charge the batteries. Bulldog wondered where the Catalina was based. Biscuit answered that the submarine Commander wanted to know that too—and then they were both wondering again what Number Four had told him. Could it have been tactical information of that sort? If Sea-Wyf had felt that the lives of her countrymen were being endangered by treacherous talk she would naturally have exclaimed against it. Although they could not discuss it at the time, it appeared that both Biscuit and Bulldog thought on very much the same lines, but neither felt satisfied by this explanation.

"Queer people, the Japs," Biscuit said. "Giving a book to starving castaways. What is it, Sea-Wyf?"

She took the parcel out of the pocket which had contained the sail and unwrapped the covering of oilcloth.

"I don't know," she said. "It is in Japanese."

"But you understand Japanese?"

"Only a very few words."

"That's clever enough. How did you come to learn even that?"

"We had a girl . . . I have known one or two Japanese," she said. She paused, then held out the book to Number Four. "Can you tell me what it is?"

He took it, evidently trying to read her expression before he glanced at the book.

"I speak a little. I went often to Japanese ports before the war and always I assisted my captains in matter of business. But I do not read it well."

He thumbed doubtfully through the pages.

"I think it is the old Japanese history, of the legends—"

"The same thing," Bulldog said. "Their whole culture is based on mythology."

"Why should he give her that?" Biscuit asked.

Number Four glanced at Sea-Wyf with inquiring, doglike eyes. She answered for him.

"I expect the Commander wanted me—all of us—to understand his people better. The Japanese are anxious to be understood. But I wonder what this says."

Inside the book she had found an envelope which contained a card with a few words written on it.

"I can guess that," Biscuit said. " 'Read it carefully, dear boy. With love from Aunt Fanny'—The Honorable Commander was not above handing on a parting present. So perhaps it's not such a significant gesture after all."

That was their longest conversation. Talking passed the time and occupied their minds with other things besides water and food. But it was dangerous, as they had discovered. Also it dried their mouths and throats, and it was tiring. They felt weak and exhausted. As the sun—and the temperature—climbed towards noon they sank into an uncomfortable lassitude, feeling too lazy even to change position when they became cramped. But the discomfort kept their minds awake —Biscuit's at least. It occurred to him that anyone at home might suppose that to travel on a raft in mid-ocean would be at least as simple and straightforward a type of life as it was possible to imagine. But here they were after less than eighteen hours together having already developed a complex society full of doubts and partly concealed passions, of dangerous stresses and strains—even a color question. There was an uncertain balance of power, with allies who were as near to quarreling as enemies, and the realization—he hoped it was a realization—that at all costs there must be no open struggle because both sides would perish if there were. It was said that people would not fight if they knew each other better. But was that so? If they knew each other's good thoughts they would also know the evil. In his mind he had already murdered everybody except Sea-Wyf—Sea-Wyf who had accepted the dangerous responsibility of handling the food and water.

The float scudded over the endless swell, now deep in a trough, then climbing the slope of sea, for a moment with a wide view from the crest, then down into another trough again.

The four human beings, their feet touching, dozed or pondered privately.

There was always the same sort of struggle, Biscuit thought —in the world, on a raft, in yourself. If you had enough to eat and drink you wanted one sort of thing, and if you didn't have enough you wanted another. In either case there was a struggle between body and mind. And the body generally won, in his experience. . . . But he hoped his mind was going to remain clear and strong. He was interested in the struggle of life, always had been. He meant to survive. The best chance would be to take things easily, not bother over much. . . . He felt asleep and dreamed vividly of food and drink.

When they woke they were all thirsty. Their backs and buttocks were sore, the sun dazzled their still sleepy eyes and their heads ached. They looked at Sea-Wyf. She answered the unspoken question. It would be better—did not they think so?—to wait until sunset before having any water. Then it would have a more lasting effect. And after all—she smiled slightly—they had each drunk about two pints already.

They accepted her judgment without question. They did not even ask how much she would let them have at sunset. It was a frightening thought that they should feel so thirsty when they had drunk the equivalent of twenty-four days' rations. Yet there was a curious relief in their predicament, in feeling themselves so dependent on a woman.

Towards evening the wind fell away entirely and the little red sail flapped idly to and fro. Number Four stood up, balancing on his single leg, one hand resting lightly on the mast. He scanned the water all round, then announced that he was going to take a swim. Would one of them go in with him while the other two kept watch for sharks? When they came out, the watchers would bathe.

"Do as you like," Bulldog said.

"You don't want to swim?"

"Not now."

Number Four grinned. "Afraid of sharks?"

"Not more than anybody else. I'll bathe when I feel inclined."

"What about you, Biscuit?"

Biscuit felt himself reacting against being addressed like that by Number Four. But having decided to take things easily he merely shook his head.

Number Four looked down at them and scowled.

"I will swim with you," Sea-Wyf said. She slipped off her smock and went over the side in her undergarment.

Number Four's face lit up with a smile as he watched her swim. Then he gave a spring and dived in.

His black head broke surface close beside her when she was about fifteen yards from the float. Her lips moved as she said something to him. He appeared to question her and she spoke again, then turned back towards the float.

Biscuit and Bulldog looked at each other questioningly.

CHAPTER FOURTEEN

THAT morning Sea-Wyf said they could have one swallow each.

She handed the water container first to Number Four, and as he held it to his lips the other two men watched his throat closely as children watch the wrists of a conjurer. They saw the muscles move several times.

"Stop!" Bulldog shouted.

"It was only one mouthful," Number Four answered, glaring.

"I saw exactly what you did. You swallowed three or four times."

"It was one swallow—little bits of the same swallow."

Sea-Wyf took the container from Number Four's hands.

"You know he did nothing wrong," she said. And when they did not express agreement, she added, "If I am to look after the stores, please do not quarrel over my suggestions."

There was a hint of appeal in her voice. Bulldog and Biscuit felt ashamed of not supporting her at once—and angry with Number Four for being the cause of the trouble.

"Naturally we will accept your judgement," Bulldog said.

And Biscuit tried to make a joke of it. "As much as you can

balance on your Adam's apple, swallow it as you please—
shall we amend it like that?" he asked.

Both he and Bulldog on that occasion took their ration at
a single gulp—and regretted it. The effect was lost so soon.
Sea-Wyf, on the other hand, swallowed it very slowly indeed.
They watched her lips and cheeks moving while she caressed
the liquid with her tongue, as a wine taster does, then let it
trickle gradually down her throat.

As they settled for the night, Bulldog felt in a state of
nervous irritation. He desperately wanted a cigarette. He
had not missed smoking before that drink in the early morning, but since then the lack had been constantly nagging at
his mind. That was not all, however. There was another
reason for his nervousness. Number Four. Whether Number
Four had taken one or three mouthfuls at sunset was of minor
importance. The point was that he might at any time drink
half a gallon before they could even try to stop him. And then
he might very well brain them with the container. He was
as powerful as the rest of them put together. And the girl
who had taken charge of the stores was in some mysterious
way in league with him, or at least sympathetic to him. If
it came to a fight the least that could happen would be that
they would all go overboard. In the water Number Four
could easily outlast them. Then he could right the float and
climb on board again. It would not be impossible to preserve
the stores—the demijohn was again attached to the life line
and the other stores could be similarly secured. So Number
Four by a single violent action could have the woman to him-

self or the stores to himself. He could do as he chose. A man
without background, with wild Negro blood running in his
veins, would be held back by no scruple. It would be crim-
inal folly to wait until he committed the crime. Then it would
be too late. The right and logical thing to do was to act first.
But how? If only he could talk to the others he knew he could
convince them. Then they could act together. But as it
was. . . . Probably there would have to be a long period of
watching and waiting, remaining very much on the alert. . . .

Bulldog began to worry about his own physical condition—
that he was so thirsty and hungry already, and that his skin
was so painful. He did not know how well he could survive
a physical ordeal. He could work with his brain, he knew, for
sixteen hours a day, for weeks and months together. But of
prolonged discomfort, thirst and hunger, he had no experience. Yet he was determined to outlive Number Four. Biscuit
too, but particularly Number Four. He would be at hand
when it came to putting that hulking body over the side.
Patience and intelligence, quickness of brain which enabled
one to act first, would carry him through. There was nothing
seriously wrong with him yet. . . . He stirred, trying to get
comfortable. But it was impossible to avoid the other feet.
In spite of his one leg Number Four took up the devil of a
lot of room.

By now it was dark except for the rag of a moon and the
infinity of dancing stars. There was practically no wind,
which was one of the reasons why they had decided not to
sail by night. The other reason had been a difficulty about

agreeing upon watches. Bulldog's instinctive objection had
been that it would be impossible to sleep while Number Four
was in charge, but fortunately it had not been necessary to
put that forward. What had they to watch for in any case?
Biscuit had asked. If bad weather blew up the float itself
would wake them soon enough. They were within inches of
the water and felt its slightest movement. The little waves
drummed loudly against the air tubes on which they rested
their heads. Besides, tired as they were, none of them really
slept. They dozed, restlessly shifted or suddenly sat up, tried
a new position on the hard floor boards and dozed again. A
small movement by anyone was enough to wake them all. . . .
So the night wore on.

Suddenly they were all upon their knees, gripping the
life line and staring about them with frightened eyes. They
must have sunk finally into a heavy sleep and now they did
not know the time except that the moon had set, which meant
it was near dawn. The float was rocking very gently. In the
starlight the water was like a sheet of dark-colored silk care-
lessly thrown down so that it was all undulations. What had
wakened them was a noise like silk being torn by hand, and
it continued, louder every second. But they could see no
cause for it.

Then the float in its slow progress rose to the crest of the
swell, and they saw a black mass bearing down on them at
speed. It was a ship without lights.

Number Four heaven himself forward, grabbed a paddle
and began to use it. Biscuit took the other, but with little

effect. As the float sank into the next trough the approaching vessel seemed for a moment less tall and solid—mast, super-structure, smoke stack. It was a warship—they could tell that by the silhouette—a destroyer probably, coming at great speed and straight at them. It seemed to climb up and up, growing in size.

Bulldog leaped to his feet, waved his arms and shouted. His voice was lost in the hiss of ripped water. The bow cut past them scarcely thirty yards away. A white explosion covered them, and the float tilted almost to its side. Biscuit got Bulldog's ankles in a rugby tackle as he was going over-board. They were conscious of a gray wall racing past them; followed by another explosion of spray. For some seconds there was complete confusion. Then the float gradually settled down, half full of water, while those aboard her coughed out the smoke which wreathed about them.

At first they thought that they were sinking and bailed with their hands, splashing the water over the side. When they discovered that the float was almost as buoyant as ever and no less stable they paused for breath.

"Have we lost anything?" Bulldog asked.

"The food and water are safe," Sea-Wyf replied. She sat huddled in the bow, her arms full.

"Not spoiled?"

"I do not think so—not if the hardtack is watertight."

"Thank God."

"There is a paddle missing," said Number Four.

They searched about them. The sail had been returned to

its pocket, wrapped round the book. The mast was safe. But one of the paddles was gone.

"Which of you had it?" Bulldog asked.

There was a pause, then Biscuit answered, "I expect it was mine."

"Why—"

"I caught hold of you, remember."

Another pause.

The girl said, "He saved your life."

"I could have swum back," Bulldog murmured.

They peered about them. It was not quite dark because of the stars and because the eastern sky was already lightening. But they could see nothing on the water.

"Whoever's fault it is we've got to find it," Bulldog said. He took up the remaining paddle and stabbed it in the water on one side, which made the float turn upon itself, accentuating the importance of the loss.

During the next half hour they stood up in turn—only one could safely stand at a time—and tried to see a little further while the others continued to bail with their hands. They did not see the missing paddle. They argued while they worked as to how it might have drifted in relation to themselves. It would have been less affected by the breeze but more so by the current, if there were one. Only Bulldog and Biscuit discussed this. The other two were silent. They were all shivering—for the first time. Feeling cold did not prevent them however from wanting a drink and—two of them at least —a smoke.

The sun elbowed itself up over the horizon, shimmering, blazing, impatient. One side of the swell glittered with color, but for a little while the other slope remained in shadow so that the ocean was a patchwork varying from dazzling to dark.

Of the warship there remained only a smudge of smoke.

"How can it have disappeared so soon?" Biscuit asked.

"From as low as we are the horizon is only about three miles away," Bulldog said.

"It must be more than that."

"No."

"In that case how can we hope to see a ship—unless it runs us down?"

"I see it," the girl exclaimed.

"What?"

"The paddle."

"Where?"

"In that direction."

"How far?"

"About—" She gave a sort of laugh—"About as far as you could hit a tennis ball with a racket."

"I can't see it."

"Not now. But I am sure I did."

There was a youthful excitement in her face which they had not seen before.

"We can't get up wind with one paddle," Bulldog said.

Like a seal Number Four went over the side and swam in the direction where the girl had pointed. His arms moved fast rhythmically, his single foot weaving to and fro as a conductor's baton beats the time.

"I thought *he* lost the paddle," Bulldog said. "I wouldn't have complained if I'd known it was you."

Biscuit made a deprecating gesture with his arms.

"He is swimming a long way," he said.

Number Four became hidden by the swell. Bulldog looked meaningly at Biscuit and slowly nodded his head. He reached for the pocket where the sail was stored.

"No!" the girl said.

"But why not set the sail now? There is a good breeze. We have got to hurry for our lives."

"No," Sea-Wyf repeated.

"He joined us without permission," Bulldog said low and vehemently. "He tried to usurp the stores. He's not one of us. He may do anything—this isn't a game of tennis. It's life or death."

He reached past her where she sat with the stores in her arms and took the sail out of the pocket.

The girl's expression was now more scared than anything else, but she kept her dark eyes full on Bulldog's face.

"For life or death he is with us on this float," she said.

"You do not understand. I have been dealing with men of his sort. The law allows killing in self-defence. Much better before the crisis comes, which it would. Then it might very well be too late. For God's sake be practical."

"There he is coming back," Biscuit said.

Bulldog began to hoist the sail.

"For God's sake—and you mean murder." The girl's voice was dangerously quiet. "If you do not lower the sail at once I will throw all the stores overboard."

Bulldog glared at her. "You silly little fool, I'll save you from yourself. Do you think you are stronger than I am?"

"Yes," she said. "I am not afraid to die, and you are." She unscrewed the stopper of the demijohn and stood up with the food in her arms.

His eyes wavered away. He lowered the sail.

"What did you say to him so privately in the water last evening?" he asked, beaten and angry, trying to hurt.

For the first time she hesitated.

"Among other things, what I have said to you. We are together on this float for life or death," she answered slowly.

Number Four swam to the float, thrusting the paddle before him like a lance. He slid over the side and crouched on the floor, dripping.

"Well done!" Sea-Wyf said warmly.

He did not answer her.

CHAPTER FIFTEEN

ALL four of them became greatly changed during the ten days which followed. This was due to the attrition caused by thirst and hunger, their cramped quarters and the callous cruelty of the sun.

Sea-Wyf changed least in appearance. Her face, though it grew thinner remained smooth, and in the bow she had a degree of privacy while the sail was set, and she used it to launder and care for her rough sailor's smock and thin, torn shift as if they were the first garments in the world. But the men, their faces covered with hair and their scant garments in rags looked like the wildest savages. That was superficial, however. The attrition went deep.

Thirst was a far greater hardship than hunger. The ordinary desire for food had soon been replaced by stomach cramps, but within a couple of days these had subsided, leaving only a dull sense of emptiness and lassitude, a strong longing but a hopeless one. Thirst on the other hand was like a flame which burned more and more consumingly. Not only in their dreams but while they were awake they imagined themselves drinking. They moved their cracked lips and tried to work their desiccated throat muscles as if they were swallowing.

During the last hour or two before sunset their eyes and thoughts were continually on the bow. Yet there was little danger of any of them taking more than the ration when the great moment came. They filled their mouths but it took time for the water to find its way down their throats.

One of the nastiest of the many unpleasant aspects of thirst was that their mouths became coated with white slime. They could scrape it off their tongue like toothpaste but it was soon replaced. It largely nullified the good effect of the daily ration. So they took the habit of rinsing out their mouths in the sea just before sunset. Then the immediate prospect of fresh water reduced the temptation to drink salt. They did swallow some but not enough to harm them.

Food, as has been said, was a matter of secondary importance. They welcomed the bean stew while it lasted because there was moisture in it. In fact Sea‑Wyf increased the ration when the stuff seemed to be going bad. But the hardtack was an entirely different matter. Bulldog and Biscuit could scarcely put it in their mouths. It absorbed at once the last traces of saliva. Number Four was the only one who persisted. He went on chewing doggedly for several minutes. Then he choked—and a cloud of dry dust blew out of his mouth.

Thus, when the stew was finished, they began to starve although they scarcely felt hungry at all.

Their cramped quarters accelerated the attrition. The almost complete lack of exercise had a bad effect upon their systems, while from sitting always in much the same positions their skins became rubbed until they developed painful sores.

SEA▸WYF

The floor boards, which consisted of lasts of wood set about an inch apart, were naturally uncomfortable—so much so that the men often turned right over and lay on their bellies, curved forward over the rubber tubes, their heads close to the water. But their tender skins were chafed even by the pneumatic tubes. They discovered each seam, each slightest inequality. And then there was the added painfulness when the rubber became hot.

The sun was an inquisitor. It generally rose with a tremendous blaze of color which painted half the sky and all the sea, suggesting that the day would be a day of doom, or dramatic in some way at least. But it always resulted in the same slow torture by heat which increased for six hours and then during a similar period gradually decreased. During perhaps half the morning Sea-Wyf got a little shade from the sail, as did the men towards evening. But for the greater part of each day the sun was mercilessly burning them. Bull-dog suffered most. His once white body looked more like that of a boiled lobster. Biscuit also suffered a good deal. Number Four, on the other hand, showed little sign of burning although he panted like a dog and seemed enervated by the heat of noon. Sea-Wyf's golden complexion protected her remarkably well. Whatever she suffered she bore it patiently, and as in the face of every other hardship remained imperturbable and unchanged.

Biscuit once said, "I understand why sailors idealize their figureheads."

But she was not passive. It was she who, by example and

suggestion, got them to follow as healthful a routine as it was possible to do. At sunrise every day they went over the side one or two at a time. They rarely swam more than a few strokes—they did not trust their strength—but they clung to the life line and let the water soak into their pores. In a queer way there was spiritual comfort in this as well as physical. For one thing it gave them a sense of privacy: it was the only time when their almost naked bodies were hidden from each other. Also it was the only time when they felt clean. Then as well as in the evening, they could wash out their mouths. And they would completely immerse themselves for as long as they could hold their breath. Biscuit said that it was like a rite of absolution.

After the morning bath the men took turns to sail the float—that was something with which to occupy one's mind. Those who were not handling the sheets let their eyes rove over the emptiness of the ocean, or leaned over the side to watch what Biscuit called the aquarium. By now there was a large number of fish swimming in the shade of the float. Most of them were tiny but a few must have weighed several pounds. Although they were remarkably tame they refused to be caught by any means at the disposal of the castaways. But they were pleasant to watch, they looked so cool.

When the weather was calm, which as a rule it was during that first ten days, Sea-Wyf would empty the hardtack into the sail pocket and soak the canvas bag. They used to wear this like a pirate's cap, in turns until it grew dry. They had nothing else except their own scant clothing with which to cover their heads, so the only other protection against sun-stroke was continually to damp their hair. This might almost be described as a full-time occupation, for it was extraordinary how quickly it got dry.

About midmorning they let some air out of the tubes—always an alarming operation. After that the day's routine focused on the still distant sunset. There was the evening bath, the food, and the great moment of the water ration. Finally they blew up the tubes again and prepared for the night. They now sailed by night as well as by day. Theoretically two of them were on watch together, but actually there was so little to do that one could doze while the other sailed and kept the look out. By a changing roster no two were consecutively paired.

This last slightly complicated arrangement was the only provision made to avoid quarrels. It was the best they could do and, in fact, all that seemed necessary. One reason for this was the rapidly enervating effects of the hardship which has been described. Their pulses beat more slowly. Although passions remained they were damped right down.

But the truly stabilizing influence was Sea-Wyf. They had been glad to place the food and water in her hands. It had appeared the natural and sensible solution to their problem. And from that moment they had become more and more dependent on her. This dependence had become stronger with hardship and their growing fear of their surroundings—for their fear increased, they never became used to their situation. Biscuit said that in the strange mixture of feeling which he had for Sea-Wyf there had been in the worst moments of the voyage a strong element of the trustful obedience of child towards mother. That she was the youngest of them made no difference. She gave them food and water and did what she could for their welfare. Her rarely spoken words were law. Whatever happened in their frightening situation, lost in a boundless, ever-moving ocean, she never changed.

The wind was almost invariably between southeast and northeast. It was rarely more than a breeze. When waves came aboard the crew bailed with their hands, finally mopping up what lay under the floor boards with the sail. They were careful to keep the craft free of salt water in the hope that there might be rain. Several times they saw rain clouds— low dark masses which trailed a fine gray curtain over the ocean as they drifted with the wind. The people in the float sailed and paddled in the attempt to intercept them. Once they came near enough to hear the rain hissing on the surface of the sea. But the cloud sailed tantalizingly away from them. They were left disheartened and exhausted.

Almost equally tantalizing were the fish which refused to be caught. They looked so cool that it seemed they must be refreshing to eat. But one morning several young sharks appeared in the aquarium, and this caused discussion of another sort. The rip of a shark's tooth would sink their craft in a moment. But no larger sharks appeared, and after a day or two the young ones left.

Then there were ships. On the first occasion it must have been a whole convoy. Had the float been ten or twenty miles farther south it would have been right in the middle of it. But as it was they only saw the patches of smoke. The ships went past hidden by the curve of the earth and the people on the float felt more desolate and lonely than ever.

The second occasion was still more distressing. It was during the brief and brilliant sunset period when the highly colored clouds which had brought no rain were camouflaging the sea with reflected reds and greens and purples. That must have been the reason why the float with its bright sail was not observed from the bridge, for the ship passed within a quarter of a mile. She was a big freighter, carrying no flag, traveling at perhaps fifteen knots. The people on the float could not stand up because it was rough but they waved frantically and tried to shout. They saw nobody at all on deck until the cook appeared from his galley. He took off his tall white hat to mop his forehead, and a ray of light caught his bald head and made it shine. He took a cigarette from behind his ear and for several minutes leaned over the rail, smoking. Then he threw the stub away and went back into the galley. The ship went on and was swallowed by the night.

The third occasion was nearly disastrous in effect for it caused a resurgence of the passions which were banked down but not far below the surface. It was dawn. Bulldog and Number Four were sharing the watch. It being Bulldog's half period of direct responsibility, Number Four had dozed off. (They all dropped asleep now, quite suddenly, like old men in armchairs.) What wind there was had become fitful, puffing from different quarters, so Bulldog had lowered the sail. With nothing to do, he also began to doze. The float like a cradle lulled them all in that hour of lowest energy.

Bulldog was wakened by a sudden tilting of the float. His sense of responsibility made him sit up and look about him, but the others, folded in strange attitudes, slept on.

He saw a single wave which must have just passed under the float and was traveling on over the oily surface, picked out by the horizontal shafts of light. Following the line of this wave he saw a ship.

From her course she must certainly have passed close by, but she was now well beyond earshot. Bulldog saw a cloud of gulls about the stern, but no sailors who might notice if he waved. He glanced at his companions. They were still asleep. He decided that it would be best to say and do nothing. Five minutes went by. He sat perfectly still, longing for the useless ship to go down over the horizon. He forced himself to look away from it.

Suddenly there was a squawk, a high-pitched mewing sound. Number Four sat up, "Birds!" he exclaimed. "That means land."

Land! They were all wide awake in a moment, peering eagerly. They saw the ship going directly away from them.

From the ship they turned to Bulldog. Number Four barked out, "You let her go. Why you let her go?"

"I could not attract their attention," Bulldog said.

"Why you didn't call us? You let her go. You want to kill us that's why you let her go."

"I tell you that they did not see—"

"What for you didn't call us? Eh? Come on!" Number Four kept thrusting out his lips, trying to moisten them with a white tongue.

"The ship has gone," Sea-Wyf said. "Let us accept that. Quarreling will not help."

The men fell silent, but there was still a sense of smoldering irritation.

"Shall we bathe?" the girl suggested.

"Before we do that I would like to try for a fish," Biscuit said. "They should be hungriest in the morning. Can I have some hardtack crumbs?"

Sea-Wyf threw the crumbs overboard and the fish came swarming to the surface, making it boil.

The paddles splashed down but killed no fish.

Then into the middle of the boiling mass a white bird dived. It came up with a half pounder in its beak, and a second later rose laboriously into the air. It tried to swallow the fish while flying but the other birds were screeching all round it and it became entirely occupied in the effort to escape. For a quarter of a minute the birds gave a display of aerobatics. Then the fish dropped, splashing into the sea only twenty yards from the float.

"Quick!" Biscuit said.

They paddled rapidly towards the fish, but before they could reach it another bird had come down like an arrow and snatched it up—to be pursued by all the rest. This continued for ten minutes at least. Sometimes a bird would get the head of the fish right into its mouth so that it looked grotesque, the tail flapping in front. Yet always in the course of the wild twists and turns which followed it was compelled to let it fall. But the float could never reach the fish before it was snatched up again. It was like a children's game played in grim earnest.

At last the humans seemed to have their chance for the fish dropped within three yards of the float. But they were very tired by then and again a bird was there before them.

This time the bird remained upon the water, and with a tremendous effort, wriggling its whole body, managed to get the fish down, all except the end of the tail. That done it remained with wings and neck extended, beak working in gasps.

Number Four's paddle came down with a crash and the bird was a mass of white feathers on the water.

All except Sea-Wyf let out the wild exultant cry of savages in a successful hunt. Their eyes were wild and their whiskered faces gloated. They tore the bird to pieces there and then. It was comparatively easy to swallow it because of the blood.

CHAPTER SIXTEEN

SEA-WYF refused to touch the bird. They saved the fish for her but she only shook her head. Her whole appearance had changed. Biscuit was shocked. He made some joke about their manners, thinking she was horrified by the way they crammed the raw flesh into their mouths. But her expression was not of horror. It was of despair. She seemed to be giving up as had so many in the lifeboats. She sank lower and lower in her place, and she muttered to herself as they had seen people do before they lost their wits and drowned themselves.

Throughout the morning she remained in much the same state, only her lips moving now and then. The men watched her with increasing anxiety, fully realizing for the first time how much they depended on her. They looked at the ocean, and at each other, fearing each other. They became overwhelmed by the hopelessness of their situation.

"Sea-Wyf," Biscuit whispered. "We need you."

It was as if she were sinking into a quicksand. Physically close though they were they could not reach her to help her out. She would have to struggle out herself, and if she sank any lower that would be impossible. They watched her lips moving and wondered what she said.

Very gradually they saw the dark, despondent eyes become sure again, the expression firm and calm. At last she held out her hand for the fish which had stuck in the bird's gullet. They gave her the battered thing and she ate it. Clearly it was a great effort for her to do this. But she chewed it slowly and swallowed it all. She smiled. She was herself again. She asked them to wash themselves and the float.

But later in the day the men quarreled and it needed all Sea-Wyf's tact to prevent violence. It was not that they had forgotten their lesson, but they could not help themselves. There was something in the air which made them restless, and they felt strong enough to express it.

Two hours before sunset Number Four said, "Let us have the water now."

Sea-Wyf shook her head with a slight smile, as a nurse refuses a patient, and Number Four acquiesced. Still more than the others he accepted whatever she said, obeying in an almost doglike way, although with the men—also in a doglike way—he was quarrelsome.

After water had been mentioned they could not think of anything except its clean feel in their mouths. The taste of the bird's blood had become foul in the slime on their tongues and palates. They longed for fresh water, not just a rinsing with salt.

Sunset colors began to light the sky. The effect was un-usual. Three-quarters of the heavens were clear except for a few scattered clouds which lit up with conventional splen-dor. But in the southwest there was a hazy mass, not quite like cloud, which did not take the light at all except at its northeastern edge where it was purple red, like a wound in black flesh. This dark mass advanced towards the sun and slid in front of it while it was still some ten degrees above the horizon. The little northern clouds went out like burning coals which have had water poured over them.

"Now!" Bulldog exclaimed.

Again the girl shook her head.

"Why? That's as good as sunset."

His sharp voice struck a cord in all of them—brittle with impatience, angry at restraint.

"Let us wait for the rain," the girl said quietly.

"It hasn't rained for a fortnight. Why should it ever rain?"

"It will tonight."

"Not on us. Last time you said it would rain we never got a drop."

"We will tonight."

"In that case let us have some water now."

Again Sea-Wyf shook her head, facing the three men.

It was not dark. Directly the mass had swallowed up the sun, three-quarters of all the stars in heaven had flashed on like electric lights, burning brilliantly against the clear dark blue. And the mass itself effused a sort of light, violet and orange. There was an extraordinary sense of tension in the air.

Looking intently at Sea-Wyf as they all were doing, Biscuit suddenly felt that he knew why she refused. During the long days with very little conversation he had sometimes half believed that he was developing a telepathic understanding of her thoughts. More than once she had said what he had some-how known she would. He had not been quite sure, had doubted it as he doubted most things about himself. But now, although she only shook her head, he was certain that he understood what puzzled and came near to infuriating the others. In their present mood she could not trust them to take one mouthful each—and if anyone drank more it would result in blows.

"She's right," he said. "The true sunset isn't for half an hour. Let's wait till then."

The others argued but at last agreed, Bulldog with an angry phrase and Number Four with a shrug.

But it was night already. The dark mass was eating up the stars one by one. If Sea-Wyf had to give out the ration in darkness it would be far more dangerous. Biscuit felt he had been wrong.

They waited in silence. The breeze had died away. There was no sound at all. The darkness spread like a thick black liquid seeping through the sky, fusing the stars. Yet it was not quite black. It became veined with curious colors—mauve and orange, violet and crimson. At first faint, these grew in intensity, silent explosions cracking the vault of cloud.

The half hour passed and another half hour. No one spoke. It felt as if any sudden noise or movement would bring the whole sky down in top of them.

The vibrations of the veins of light had become more violent. Now and then the sky seemed to smash into pieces, showing a blazing fire behind as if it were hell up there, not heaven. Next moment the obscuring mass healed itself. But the next, fierce lights were flashing through a hundred cracks again.

Still there was no sound and no rain. The murk had spread over the whole sky, and the occasional convulsions of light were so brilliant that the three men and the woman were blinded. They could not see each other crouching together in an area six feet by four.

They heard growling noises—deep, menacing but indistinct. Here and there about them were splashes as big as if fish were jumping. But they felt no rain. They could see nothing either in the darkness or in the blinding light. The prickings of their sunburned skins became so painful that they had to move, but this only intensified the irritation. They wanted to strike out, to jump up, to run. The growling noises were more frequent. There was also a crisp whisper like dead leaves in wind which became harder and harder to bear although somehow it was not loud. But the separate grumblings became louder. They coalesced and swelled and went on swelling into an intolerable vibrant din with which the dashing, darting veinings of brilliant light kept time . . . .

And then the whole thing burst with a crash which numbed the senses.

Down came the water. Rain is not the word. It was so different from rain that for a little while the frightened people crouched away from it as from a storm wave. It was only when it forced its way between their lips as it did into everything else that they realized it was fresh water. Then they put back their heads and opened their mouths wide. It beat upon their faces. It streamed from their hair, over their cheeks and closed eyes, it poured like a running tap from their noses. Their whiskers and moustaches dripped with it. It battered them, but they held their cupped hands under their chins to catch more. At first they could scarcely swallow. Then their throats became lubricated and they gulped it down—on and on and on. The thirst they had felt when they found the submarine had been nothing. Now their sand-dry bodies seemed able to absorb an infinite quantity, and still they wanted more. They even dropped on their knees to suck up the water in greater quantities from the bottom of the float. They drank and drank under the deluge until at last it was impossible to swallow any more. They were still thirsty but there was no room for any more inside them.

The waterfall continued and they discovered they were cold. The sea when it had splashed them or they had gone into it in the past had been warm. But this was cold. They huddled, shivering, sitting on the edge of the float with their feet in water and their ears full of the noise, which was like a cataract. There was no more lightning or thunder, only water and the noise it made pouring down into the sea.

Gradually the descending water changed to ordinary rain which fell more and more lightly until at last it stopped. And simultaneously the sky was clear. The dark mass did not drift away. It had come down upon the ocean and there was nothing left of it. The stars lit up again and in the wonderfully clear air they shone more brilliantly than they had ever done before. The ocean appeared limitless under their light, a vast plane of space.

But on the tiny extraneous speck which floated in the

middle of it the human beings were very cold indeed. They were not used to cold and in any case their resistance was low. Their craft had changed from a float to a water trough three parts full. But they could not bring themselves to jettison their priceless cargo. So they sat with their feet in it and shivered.

Then Sea-Wyf handed round some hardtack. The canvas bag had been practically untouched during the preceeding ten days so they felt justified in having several ounces each. But, damp though it was, they found it difficult to chew because their gums were sore. It took them a long time to masticate and swallow it. This helped to pass the night.

At last the sun came up. Within a matter of minutes they ceased to be cold. They became hot and longed for shade.

They discussed what they should do with the abundance of fresh water. "We've won a pool all right," Biscuit said, and laughed at his own joke. They all felt lightheaded. They replenished the container. The demijohn had not yet been broached. There was nowhere to put any more so they left it swilling about in the bottom of the float. There was a slight danger in this for it made them lower in the water and presumably it was a strain on their frail craft. But they decided to drink it as quickly as they could. The only embarrassment was that they had constantly to be going over the side because their bodies could not hold the liquid for any time at all.

Their luck appeared radically to have changed, for that afternoon another gull appeared. It may have been one of

the same flock, which had failed to catch up again with the
ship it had been following and had been battered by the
storm. At any rate it was completely exhausted. It settled on
the float and was killed without difficulty. No longer raven-
ous they ate it slowly, even with a hint of manners. Sea-Wyf
accepted a piece. They talked together politely, and laughed.
Their skins were clean of salt, perfectly clean and fresh for
the first time. They were all elated, amicable and hopeful. If
only they had a wind they would soon get somewhere.

Towards evening a breeze blew up—a fair wind from the
east. The brave little float began to trundle rather heavily
along, making swishing and gurgling noises. . . . The wind
increased and waves began to come over the side. That was
serious. In an attempt to prevent it the sail was lowered. But
the wind grew stronger and waves still leaped on board, more
and more of them. Within an hour the water in the float was
not only brackish but dangerously high. It was necessary to
bail, to splash the water out more quickly than it came in.
Without a sail the float spun round and round and tipped at
every angle. They were seasick.

After sunset the wind dropped away—but not as low as
their spirits. Their net gain had been half a container of fresh
water—a few mouthfuls each. What was the good of going
on trying, torturing themselves? They sat brooding in the
darkness, and when their legs became intangled in the pool
in the middle of the floor they kicked out petulantly. They
hated each other and, very nearly, life itself.

CHAPTER SEVENTEEN

"HAVE you *no* idea where we were in the *San Felix?*" Bulldog asked Number Four. His voice was angry. "Oh, I realize that wasn't your job. But you must have seen the chart or heard the Captain say something. Didn't you?"

Number Four shook his head in surly silence.

"Then can't you tell by the sun or the stars? I should have thought any professional sailor, even a pur—even one with your job—would have picked up some knowledge of navigation."

"That is not fair," Sea-Wyf said.

"Take his side as usual! What is fair in any case?"

Bulldog turned to Biscuit. His eyes, which were red and inflamed, looked furiously angry.

"If only one knew how long we must keep going, where to steer—anything, one could put up with it. It's the complete uncertainty that gets on one's nerves."

"I never thought of that," Biscuit said.

There was a bitter satisfaction in making an old joke which he knew Bulldog did not see.

That was really the only point in making jokes, to annoy Bulldog.

They heard a faint drumming sound, and after searching the brassy vault of sky at last picked out the aircraft. There was a whole squadron of them, very high up—twenty thousand feet or more. At three hundred miles an hour they had a chance of getting somewhere. But on the float. . . . Airplanes and ships, they went about their own business seeing nothing else. They only accentuated the utter loneliness.

"We better paddle till the wind comes," said Number Four.

"If you had any idea in which direction to paddle it would be a help—"

"We have been going westward all the time," Sea-Wyf said. "Surely we should continue to go west."

"Go west is right," Biscuit muttered. He felt utterly tired of it all. Danger and hardship which are supposed to bring out the best in people had only made them childishly petulant and selfish—all except Sea-Wyf, of course. Without her they would have killed each other long before, and perhaps that would have been the best thing. On the day of the submarine they had thought they knew what privation was. Innocent fools! But they knew now. There was another eight hours before Sea-Wyf would give them a mouthful of water —or two if she felt generous. That would be over in a few seconds, and there would be twenty-four hours to wait for the next reminder of past pleasures. Then another twenty-four hours and another—on and on until they died in agony. . . . He looked at Sea-Wyf. She was mopping up the last of the salt bilge water with the sail, wringing it out over the side. She might have used the sail for shelter but instead she was being useful. She was always being useful, taking the side of anyone who looked as if he were being bullied. Chiefly Number Four. For himself, Biscuit, she did not seem to care. He was not jealous, but it seemed so silly. He was the only one who understood her.

About noon Biscuit felt that the heat was quite intolerable and without saying anything to anybody slipped over the side. He began to swim away from the float which was rocking on the now oily swell. The water was gentle and cool. It had never caressed his limbs in quite the same way before. In a moment it seemed to wash away all his troubles and unhappiness. Even the sun which had been burning him so cruelly felt quite pleasant on his wet head. Everything was bright and blue and friendly. . . . He swam slowly on.

"Biscuit," called Sea-Wyf's voice. "Biscuit."

He swam on. He had not realized before that he was going to end it all, but now he knew that he was going to do just that. He swam on. He had a sense of exultation.

"Biscuit, come back!"

There was appeal in her voice. She minded. It was pleasant that she minded. But how utterly delightful was the soft, clean feel of the sea.

Some lines of poetry came into his head.

> Now more than ever seems it rich to die
> To cease upon the midnight with no pain—

It wasn't midnight. It would not be the same thing at night.

The dark was frightening. But now, for the first time since the sinking, he had no fear at all.

The ocean and the sunlight are my friends—was that a quotation too or had he made it up? He felt himself a poet at that moment, in tune with the universe.

"Biscuit!"

"Good-by," he muttered.

"Sharks!"

He stopped swimming.

"Sharks!" They were all shouting.

His entrails violently contracted and then seemed to turn to water. He splashed around. For an agonizing moment he could not see the float. Then it was heaved up by the swell and he saw it—unbelievably small in the middle of an ocean unbelievably large and hostile. He struck out towards it, using every ounce of his strength.

As he approached the float he saw that they were not looking at him but over his head. He had no strength left but something else drove his limbs. Hands took him by the shoulders and pulled him on board.

"Three, four, five of them," Bulldog was saying.

"Six," said Number Four. "Here they come."

The sharks had been cruising round the float, only their fins showing. These looked something like the sails of toy yachts except that they were black. One had turned inwards from its circular course and was coming towards the float. Bulldog and Number Four knelt on the side tubes, each grasping a paddle like a club and holding onto the life line with his other hand. Biscuit was too exhausted to do anything. Sea-Wyf knelt on the floor boards, very still.

The shark went by like a torpedo a few yards away, then rejoined the others in their circular course which gradually spiraled inwards. Another turned, and went deep under the float. A third passed close by, just below the surface, moving very slowly. They could see it clearly—the blunt snout, the pale expressionless eyes, the long lithe body and the powerful tail which gently undulated. It was inexpressibly sinister. The crowd of fish which had gathered under the float came boiling to the surface in a panic.

"We shouldn't have killed that sea bird," Number Four said in a broken voice.

"Nonsense!" Bulldog was thinking of the small scraps which had been thrown overboard and which could scarcely have attracted sharks.

"It's bad luck to kill sea birds."

Another shark nosed past. They were all close by now.

"Bad luck! It was you killed them," Bulldog said.

Number Four dropped his paddle. His face was gray, his eyes miserable.

"I killed 'em. Bad luck to kill sea birds," he kept muttering.

Sea-Wyf, still on her knees, picked up the paddle and handed it to Biscuit. He took it automatically but he did not feel he had the strength to use it. The superstition was absurd, but voiced just then, the fear of consequence so evident, it had a numbing effect.

Next moment the attack was launched. The sharks came

racing in from every side and scores of little fish rose straight into the air in front of them. The water seethed. As the sharks charged they rolled over, showing their cream white bellies, their miserable inverted U-shaped mouths. They struck the float as they went by, making it jump and spin, their skins scraping the rubber with a rasp like sand paper. They turned with a great sweep of their tails and came back. They went deep and came up so fast that they broke surface. Snouts, tails, fins, jumping fish, seething water, the float bouncing and tilting — there was no question of those on board defending themselves. They clung to the life lines, thrown from side to side so that they bumped and kicked each other.

As suddenly as the attack had started it was over. The sharks remained for a little longer near the float, cruising to and fro, deep down and indistinct, like the ghosts of wicked submarines. But soon they disappeared altogether. The water, of course, had immediately calmed down. All the little fish had gone. The float was rising and falling very gently on the swell like the chest of a person who is just alive. All around as far as it was possible to see there was nothing except the oily undulation of water; above only the burning-glass of sky with the blazing focus point in the center.

"They were not attacking us. They were fishing," Bulldog said. His red face was streaming with sweat and his inflamed eyes looked horribly painful.

"We are leaking," Biscuit said. He was too tired for fear. There was a good deal of water in the bottom of the float.

They bailed and mopped it out as quickly as they could, then knelt anxiously watching the dry bottom.

It remained dry.

"Brave little float," Biscuit murmured. Then, because he was ashamed of himself for his past weakness, he made an attempt at lightness.

"Evidently the second seabird canceled out the first."

He glanced at Sea-Wyf who was the only one who ever smiled at his jokes. She was silently weeping.

"What's the matter?" he asked.

"The sharks will not come back now the fish have gone," Bulldog told her.

Sea-Wyf controlled herself. "I have lost the water container," she said.

They stared at her, unable to believe her words.

"The demijohn was tied," she went on. "The hardtack is in the pocket with the pump. I was holding the container, but it went overboard. The biscuit tin also."

If anybody else had said that, or even if she had said it in another way, or tried to conceal it, there would have been furious denunciations. But as it was she touched something gentle which was still in their hearts. Bulldog gathered up the bodies of a dozen little fish which had jumped on board and awkwardly, handed them to her. Biscuit said that the loss did not matter. And in fact it did not really seem to him to matter. They would die a little sooner, that was all.

"Will one of you take charge of the stores?" Sea-Wyf asked.

"No!" Biscuit and Bulldog answered together. The suggestion alarmed them.

They sat in silence for half an hour or more. There did not seem anything to do or say.

"That was the second sea bird!" Number Four shouted.

Sea-Wyf faced him, suddenly roused. "No. It is wrong to say such things."

"It was!" he shouted wildly. "It was. None of you understand."

CHAPTER EIGHTEEN

BULLDOG had behaved better than any of them during the shark attack, but it took the most out of him. That night he was too tired to sleep. He sat worrying over their position, their different personalities, the possible dangers as well as those which were inevitable. He could not take his eyes from the sea and the occasional flashes of phosphorescent light when some unknown creature broke the surface. But when at last he fell asleep it was to drop into so deep a slumber that even the rising sun did not disturb it.

The others sat and looked at him. They were all permanently tired those days and any excuse was good enough to postpone the morning chores.

Bulldog was not a pretty sight. His chest and drawn-in belly were covered with small sores. The skin of his face—what was visible between the whiskers—was patched with black and red. His cheeks were sunken. His tightly closed mouth looked more than ever severe. The semicircles of his eyelids were framed by a yellowish secretion which seemed to gum them shut. . . . But Biscuit was only looking at him because it made him wonder what he himself was like in appearance. He knew that his ribs stood out like bars, that his legs were absurdly thin, that he had red pimples all over and boils in the most awkward places. But he could not imagine his own face. He had never seen it covered with hairs. . . .

Biscuit looked at the others. Number Four's body was as lean as it could be. But the muscles were still there, (he had one leg less to feed) and there were no ugly spots upon his dark skin. His face was less changed than caricatured. The Negroid qualities were accentuated, the European had faded. The whites of the deep-sunken eyes were particularly striking. The bones of the face, cheek and jaw bones, stood out. The lips, no longer fleshy but still large, protruded. He had developed a mannerism which suggested that he was sucking at something, reminiscent of a goldfish testing the sand in its bowl, sucking it in and blowing it out. Not an attractive habit. But the most striking thing about him was his hair which with its minute and intricate crinkles was as neat as if he had just come from the barber.

Sea-Wyf was the same as ever, thank God—or so it seemed to Biscuit. Her face showed suffering but nothing could alter for long the serenity of her expression. And as much as possible she kept her body covered.

Bulldog stirred. His face twitched. He rubbed his closed eyelids with a hand, then opened them, and blinked.

"I have been such a long way," he murmured. "Miles and miles over the moor. I shot as much as I can carry . . . But I can't find the house."

For a few seconds longer he lay wearily blinking at the hard blue sky. Then his expression changed. He sat up quickly. He glanced about him, at the sea, heaving and limitless; and for a moment there was something like terror in his face.

"A damn fool dream," he muttered angrily.

Sea-Wyf cleaned his eyes with a rag from her shift moistened with fresh water. He grumbled, saying it was waste, but gave in to her. The other two watched silently.

That day they were all more silent and apparently more thoughtful than usual. Bulldog was worried by his experience. It did not make sense. In a somewhat different way Biscuit was worried by it too. Beyond their other fears they must all have been preoccupied for some time by the fear of madness. They had seen symptoms of it in each other. Sea-Wyf's behavior after the killing of the first sea bird. Biscuit swimming away. Number Four overcome by superstition. Now Bulldog's dream remaining after he had woken up. . . . They had all had dreams—sometimes they had described them, for almost invariably they were of such delightful things as water and fruit and shade. What none of them had talked about was that dreams became more vivid as privation increased. Now Bulldog of all people had bridged the gap. Biscuit at least could imagine himself doing the same. But he must not, would not. There madness lay. Looking at Sea-Wyf, he knew that she was thinking on the same lines. She had recovered from her lapse. So had he—after all it had consisted of nothing more than swimming too far because it was enjoyable. Bulldog similarly was explaining away to himself that inconsequent remark. The others might go mad, but not oneself—never.

In the afternoon, fortunately, the wind blew up and the float began once more to trundle along under its little red sail. It had a character of its own, the float. It was a fussy little duck, but a brave one. It thrust its pneumatic bosom towards the horizon which never came any nearer just as if it were crossing a pond. They heard the water bubbling under it and frothing up astern. That was the sane and sensible thing to do, to push on with all speed, without thinking.

The wind did not always blow from the same direction but, as the Japanese interpreter had said, land was all around. Sometimes—for very little reason—they were all optimistic; just as—for as little direct cause—they changed to gloom. For instance, when Sea-Wyf brought out the fish the men's whiskered faces lit up with smiles. It looked such a lot—like a miracle. But when they tried to eat the sticky, tasteless flesh they were nauseated. To get that down they needed far more water than she allowed them. In spite of their loss she had increased the ration to three mouthfuls, but even that was not enough. They were miserable and hopeless again.

Yet when a flock of flying fish came ricocheting along at dawn one morning, and two of them struck the sail and fell into the float, these same men laughed with excitement. . . . They put the little things into their mouth, to eat them quickly before they dried—and the endless bones stuck to the slime of their tongues and palates. It was horrible.

But they got some rain. The first fell four or five days after the electric storm. (They had ceased to calculate time with any certainty, there were only outstanding events.)

SEA⋅WYF

This rain came in the night. They woke to find their faces wet and water in their mouths—so their dreams merged into reality. The rain was nothing like as abundant as in the electric storm but it came down heavily for half an hour while they caught it in their mouths, sucked it from their whiskers, licked it off their arms, trapped it in their hands. When the rain had stopped falling they went on their knees and sucked up the water from between the floor boards. In the darkness they bumped into each other. They became excitedly angry, cursed and shouted. The water was brackish because although the floor had been dry it was crusted with salt. But brackish water was better than sea water, or nothing at all, and they went on filling themselves to the neck from fear that waves would come over the side—for it was quite rough. They were still busily groveling at dawn. Then Number Four did something which made it impossible for them to drink any more, and there was a furious battle of words. It is fairly certain that blood would have been spilled, perhaps with fatal results, if Sea-Wyf had not gone on her knees between the men. She had already replenished the demijohn to the brim, she said, by guiding rain into it with her hands. Without a sign of emotion she told Number Four to mop out the float. After some moments of scowling silence he obeyed.

This scene exhausted them, as did any exertion. They lay back in their places while the float bustled merrily along. Sea-Wyf gave them some hardtack which they sucked and nibbled at until at last it dissolved. Each tried to make his own piece last longer than that of anybody else. They

163

watched each other out of the corners of their eyes as dogs do when eating.

Twice during the following week they got rain, on both occasions in daylight. These showers were light and short, but provided enough to form saliva and make it possible to eat. There were no more angry scenes. Yet, in a way, shouting and cursing were better than brooding silence. From lack of energy, wordy quarrels burnt themselves out almost immediately. But each man when he brooded began to think that the others were gathering their strength for a sudden outburst of physical violence.

This was particularly the case during the periods of calm. Then even the noble little float seemed futile, the heat was doubly oppressive, the hours of waiting for the water ration stretched eternally, everything was more of a strain.

Number Four had withdrawn into himself. It had started when Sea-Wyf had told him he was wrong to insist upon the superstition about the bird. After she had made him mop out the float he had seemed to become more than ever burdened by his grievances. His eyes, with those startling whites, were continually watching one or another of his companions. His lips kept up their pouting—sucking movement. But otherwise he scarcely moved. And as the days passed the rest began to feel that the crisis, if crisis it were, was receding with his strength. He had given up.

One calm morning—it must have been eight or nine days after the shark attack—they went overboard for a bath. They did not swim any distance now, but put their heads back and floated, letting the water fondle their stiff, sore limbs. Number Four went in, and was out again first, Sea-Wyf last. Biscuit and Bulldog lingered in the water beside her, making the most of the cool comfort.

To anybody else the two ends and sides of the float would have appeared identical. But to those who had used it for so long their own places were individual and particular. They had each a strong proprietary sense about them. Therefore when Sea-Wyf climbed out of the sea and found Number Four in the bow she was shocked and startled.

"You are in my place," she said, kneeling in the middle.

He shook his head, his deep white-ringed eyes hypnotically fixed upon her face.

"But you are!" She tried to laugh.

Again he shook his head, self-satisfied and sure.

The other two men were astride the side tubes. Their instinct told them that this was serious trouble. But they still glowed with the brief refreshment of their bath.

"Please let me have my place."

Sea-Wyf, her hair tousled like a boy's, her face with shining pearls of water on it, her black eyes glowing, was still an attractive, an appealing, figure. But Number Four only slightly shook his head, his expression set as a statue's.

"Come on, you know you are in the bow," Bulldog said sharply.

Damn fool, Biscuit thought. Now we are committed. He had known that Sea-Wyf did not want them to interfere in this because it would only make it harder for her. But Bulldog had not known. They were dealing with a man who was on a tight rope above the gulf of madness. Biscuit felt sure of that.

Bulldog in another way now realized his mistake, for Number Four took no notice of him at all. Bulldog wondered what to do. He could not forcibly remove the man. Apart from the near certainty of capsizing the float he had not half his strength. He could not have lifted a passive body let alone a fighting one.

There was a puff of wind. Automatically Biscuit gathered in the sheet cords so that the red triangle filled. But the float would not sail properly with a more than double weight in the bow. It was as if for the first time it showed disapproval of its crew.

Bulldog was still glowering at Number Four. Number Four was still holding Sea-Wyf with his eyes.

"I take charge of rations now," the mulatto said, patting the demijohn and the pocket which contained the hardtack. He grinned at Sea-Wyf.

"You all agreed that I should look after them," she said quietly.

He grinned again, his lips parting, showing his white teeth, and the gums which were a mess of sores.

"But you lost some," he said. "You are only a woman. It is mine. I take it now."

"Please!" Sea-Wyf said.

She was using her only weapons, her soft voice and her eyes. But they had no effect. Number Four looked away from her and settled himself more comfortably, spreading his arms to guard the rations. The other two men could do nothing and they knew it.

Sea-Wyf continued to kneel in front of the dusky god who now held all their lives in his hands. He glanced up at her slyly. Then he unscrewed the stopper of the demijohn and took a drink, quite slowly but watching the others while he did so. Then he settled down again, smiling, passing his tongue over his lips. The other two men were tense upon the side tubes. But they felt more hopeless than determined, almost resigned.

Sea-Wyf still knelt in front of Number Four. The others could not see her face.

"Tell me, how was it that you lost your leg?" she asked.

Her voice was soft and interested. Number Four started and looked at her suspiciously.

"Why you want to know?" he demanded.

"I have always wanted to know. I have been afraid to ask. But now I think you will tell me."

His eyes were trying to bore into her face. At last the suspicion faded.

"I tell you," he said. " 'Nother little drink and I tell you. You want water?"

She shook her head.

"I only want to hear about your poor leg."

Number Four drank long and slowly, then replaced the stopper.

"I was a little kid," he said, "six years old. I was playing

with the other kids in the road. They all liked me then. 'Long
came a big automobile—shining like a star, dust flying all
round. Other kids ran. I just stared. It went right over me."

"How terrible! Could not the car stop?" Sea-Wyf asked.

"Sure it stopped—bit farther on. There was a fat man with
a white face and spectacles looking down at me. He had a
cigar in his hand. I smell that cigar. He came and saw me in
the hospital—petted my head and gave me ten dollars. That's
all I got out of white men. Ten dollars."

"Could not they give you an artificial leg?" Sea-Wyf
asked.

"No. No, they couldn't do that," Number Four was becoming excited. "It wasn't just the leg. Hips went too. I was
in the hospital long time on and off. Operations. One lasted
five hours. That's where I started to get my learning, in the
hospital. There was a woman bit like you came and taught
me—"

"I am very glad somebody was kind to you," Sea-Wyf said.

"Kind? Wait till I got out of the hospital. Wait till I grew
up. Nobody was good to me—white or colored. And I was
a cripple. But the rest of me got strong, look—"

He held up his arms as a boxer does in acclamation and the
muscles writhed about the bones.

"Sailors was the nearest kind," he went on. "Sailors know
cripples are the poor of God. It's only 'cos they know it's
bad luck not to, but they'll never harm a cripple. That's why
I turned sailor, superior sort of sailor. But passengers—"

"I want to be kind to you," Sea-Wyf said.

There was a pause.

While he had been telling his story Number Four had been pathetic. But now a look of extraordinary cunning came over his face.

"Real kind?" he asked.

"I will do everything I can for you," the girl said earnestly. She had dropped her eyes at last and seemed to speak more to herself than to him. "If God grants us a future I will do more."

"You swear it?"

"I will do what I have said if you will do something for me."

"What's that?"

"Go back to your own place and let me have mine. Let me take charge of the rations again."

Number Four leaned forward, closely examining her downcast face.

"I do that and you'll be real kind to me?"

The girl nodded.

The cunning expression on the mulatto's face changed to one of gloating satisfaction. At that moment, when the original crisis was suddenly resolved, the two white men came nearest to striking him. But they did not do so. They despised themselves as cowards for not doing so.

"It's a deal," said Number Four, and grasped her limp hand. Pulling himself along with his arms, trailing his leg, he moved to the stern. The float, properly trimmed again, began immediately to sail true and fast. But as he continued to watch Sea-Wyf the look of exultant satisfaction was still upon the dusky, big-lipped face, and until it was wiped away there could be no peace on that crowded world six feet by four in area.

CHAPTER NINETEEN

THE wind, after the preliminary puffs, grew steadily stronger. The silky surface of the ocean first became corrugated into millions of tiny wrinkles. These ripples coalesced into larger mounds of moving water. After a while, the wind continuing to increase, these mounds—always moving —became fewer still and still larger. They grew into waves with white crests which were blown forward by the wind. Brave, lively waves—but they had not yet supplanted the wide, kindly old swell from which they were drawn. It was their distant ancestor which had survived the last calm—perhaps a dozen other calms and a dozen little blows—and would continue to form the general pattern of the ocean unless these waves which moved in a slightly different direction became larger than it. They looked virile enough but they were still young and cheerful.

Those were Biscuit's thoughts. They were forced. He was compelling himself to pay imaginative attention to the rest of the universe and forget the six feet by four of his immediate surroundings. There black silence reigned.

The great clouds were forming into ranks. In the east there was no clear horizon but a hazy line which stirred and spread. The waves were joining forces and becoming more powerful.

But they were still gay in the sunlight. Their plumed crests formed rainbows. The spray stung like a boisterous kiss. A score of flying fishes rose like a covey of brightly colored partridges and biplaned a hundred yards or so into the wind while a school of beautiful blue dorado jumped for them, looking like heraldic dolphins tired of their sculptor's poses and sprung into lively life.

The float tilted on its nose, then its tail, and gurgled with amusement. Its rubber crinkled as a face does in a smile. But there was danger in this sort of play, danger everywhere. The flying fish, however gracefully, had been fleeing for their lives. So were they, humans. The dolphins lost their prey, joined the float and went bounding along beside this new fat friend. But the float could not dive through the waves. It had to try to jump them. Invariably it tripped on top and came down staggering into the trough. Light and brave though it was it did not belong to the same element.

It was in the afternoon that the character of the wind changed. There appeared a snake-like viciousness in the hissing crests which licked the float. A big ship would have steamed on unnoticing. Her sailors would have called this just a good Trade Wind blow. But the float veered and lurched so that those on board had to snatch out and hold on for their lives.

The sense of common danger grew until it was at least something of a bond. When Sea-Wyf was thrown across the floor board, Number Four took down the mast and stretched the sail and stay cords across and across the float, from one life line to the other, bootlace fashion—and the others helped him. But they still hated him while they helped for he was in an exultant state, like drunkenness, beyond fear. He shouted a song into the wind.

When the cords were arranged the crew were underneath a sort of net which yet permitted a certain amount of movement. Movement was necessary because they had to bail, cupping their hands and throwing the water upwards to be carried away by the wind. They did not know what would happen if the float became completely full. Biscuit shouted— it was impossible to be heard except by shouting—that they ought to blow up the tubes to the limit. This they did with great difficulty and some danger for it involved leaning over the side.

Sea-Wyf gave them all a drink and some hardtack. Quite a lot of water was lost for it was impossible to handle the heavy demijohn safely. It rapped them painfully on the lips and teeth. There was no thought of an exact ration. They were living for the moment. This refreshment, and the safety preparations which had gone before it, occupied a long time, several hours. Because they were continually being thrown about it needed a great struggle, and the choice of the right moment, to make any particular movement. And all the time they had to bail. Before they realized it, night was coming on.

For a little while the dolphins still accompanied them, going through the waves like phosphorescent torpedoes. But soon they vanished in the general chaos.

The night was a long agony, so long that even the possibility of daylight was forgotten. They were made giddy and dazed by the continual irregular movement, but they were not actually seasick. They had little enough to be sick on, it is true, but they did not even retch. Probably this was because they were too preoccupied with holding on, half numbed with fear.

Several times during the night there were rain squalls. But the men did not drink much. It was too painful to face the wind. And the rain was bitterly cold. They preferred to snuggle down in the sea water which swilled about inside the float and which was lukewarm by comparison.

They had ceased to bail. The float spilt out a good deal of water of its own accord when it tripped over a crest. At other times it was filled by a single shower of spray. Then for a while it felt as if they were in the ocean itself. But the sail and the laced lines kept them on board.

Without any of the usual preliminaries of dawn the sun was up, glaring from the wind-polished sky. The float was at the bottom of a valley. In front was a steep hill of water which stretched quite straight as far as they could see to either side. Behind was another, steeper hill with spray blowing off the top of it as snow blows off an alpine ridge. The float could not escape this following hill. It seemed to be drawn backwards towards it. Above the stern hung thousands of tons of seething water on the point of rushing down in a green avalanche. But the float, tilted at a sharp angle, continued to be pulled backwards up the slope. It reached the crest. There the full force of the wind struck it, spun it, rocked it. For a moment there was a view of an infinity of parallel lines—similar white-capped ridges of water with deep wide valleys in between. This view was lost as the float receded, backwards or sideways, down the slightly more gentle reverse slope of the hill. At the bottom, for a moment, it floated horizontally, and the people aboard it saw another long hill of water towering up astern.

That experience was repeated every two or three minutes throughout the day.

There were variations—always unpleasant—when a squall blew up. They saw these squalls coming when they were on a crest, dark hazy lines which came out of the horizon and raced the waves, rapidly coming closer until suddenly they struck. Then the surface was all whirlpools and the air was so full of spray that it was almost impossible to breathe. Also the crests were sometimes corkscrewed up into jagged pinnacles which hissed as they moved, tottered and crashed down. When part of one of these struck the float it was driven under for a moment. Only its small rounded shape, its inoffensive lightness, saved it from complete destruction. It rode over almost everything, or slipped aside.

In one squall the float was tilted at so steep an angle that the demijohn went overboard. Biscuit who was nearest tried to pull it in again by the cord to which it was attached to the life line. As he leaned over the side he saw—or thought he saw—that the life line itself was about to be ripped away by the weight of the suspended demijohn. The life line was attached to a series of loops sewn or gummed—he did not know which—onto the rubber. If the strained loop were sewn, and if it tore out, a hole would be formed. He had got the demijohn to the surface, but could do no more. He could lift it in water but not, with the increased gravity, in air. If he let go the loop would be pulled out. He imagined the float collapsing in a moment. He panicked. He untied the handle of the demijohn. He clung on to it, shouting for help. But the others could not understand. He held on as long as he could. But his head went under a wave while his mouth was open. He choked and let go.

The others showed no reaction. They were too far gone.

The second night descended. The wind howled, the waves hissed and stung and crashed on board in darkness. Through the film of spray the stars were shining. The storm must have reached its peak in a furious squall which struck them about midnight, but the exhausted, battered crew were beyond realizing this. And yet Biscuit at least was conscious that he was going to survive. He had had that feeling all the time. He did not much want to live but he knew that he was going to survive.

When the sun at last rose again the waves were still huge but they had lost their purpose. They only traveled with what was left of their momentum. They rose and fell aimlessly. If anything the result was still more uncomfortable for the prostrate people in the float. But as the morning wore on and the sun climbed higher, unobscured by spray, they realized that the storm was over. Curled up in the water under the lacing cords they slept.

They woke in the evening. They rubbed their faces which were caked with salt and opened their eyes with their fingers. They stretched their stiff limbs and blinked at each other. Automatically, with slow, painful movements, they began to bail. Sea-Wyf took out the bag of hardtack. She extracted two large pieces. She tried to break them, and failed. She handed them to Biscuit. He was almost as weak as she was, but at last, by striking the pieces against his knees, he managed to divide them fairly. He handed the ration round and when he had done so found that he had two left, one for himself, and another.

"Why?" Bulldog asked.

"I—I thought there were five of us," Biscuit answered.

He read the look on Bulldog's face. Sea-Wyf looked at him queerly. Why the devil had he thought that? He passed a miserable night in which every dozing dream was another hallucination.

Dawn came with tropical suddenness, but the four exhausted people were slow to rouse themselves. They lay with their legs intertwined and the upper halves of their bodies draped one way or another over the side tubes. The movements of the float, slightly rocking and very slowly turning, were soothing as a hammock. The balmy morning breeze added to this effect. The sea which mildly rose and fell without a break upon its surface was unrecognizable as the terrible thing on which they had existed for two days. They had the feeling that by some magic they had been transported a thousand miles to a place where there was peace, and all they wanted was to go to sleep again.

As the float slowly gyrated, Sea-Wyf's neck twisted in the opposite direction. She pulled her feet under her and got upon her knees. For some time she remained thus, gazing over the water. Then she raised her eyes to the sky where great cumulous clouds were floating, and Biscuit saw upon her face an expression which did not belong to this world. As far as he felt anything he felt sad. The girl's lips moved but made no sound. He knew what that meant.

After a little while she said, very quietly, "I see trees."

"Where?" Biscuit asked.

"Rising from the sea."

The extraordinary light was still in her eyes. Poor Sea-Wyf.

But he heaved himself up, and sure enough there were palm trees. If he had been the first to notice them he would have said nothing, for they appeared to be growing out of the ocean. He shook the other two men, and pointed. Their mental reactions were as slow as their stiff, awkward movements. Yes, there were trees, and down wind. But the smiles came only gradually and doubtfully. The men began with scarcely a hint of excitement to unlace the safety net of stay cords.

But the excitement was there and it grew as they worked until it took possession of them. Their hands were trembling, they were shouting and cackling with laughter and tumbling in each other's way as they hoisted the sail. Tears streamed down their faces. Their quarrels and differences were quite forgotten. The only thing they thought about was land.

The float began to move. They still had the paddles. They had been stowed between the tight bulge of the side tubes and the floor boards. Using one of these as a rudder they steered towards the palm trees. The float seemed at first to travel fast, water bubbling under the bow. Brave little thing! They felt a warm affection for it. But the palm trees remained a long way off, ten miles at least. There is nothing more exasperating than a wind which dies away when you most want it. Having blown too strongly for two days it was now only a miserable breeze. But they needed one paddle to steer with, and the other was no use alone. They had to wait, impatiently. They wondered what the island might be. They discovered that they knew next to nothing about the Indian Ocean. Even Number Four only knew the main islands and this, small and flat as an inverted plate, could not be one of those. But that mattered very little. It was land. Solid land. Would there be people on it?

From the crests of the swell they made out the bulge of sand and scrub from which the trees sprouted. In front they saw a curved line of brilliant whiteness. They also thought they made out the masts of a ship. Yes, they were sure of it. So there must be people on the island. They discussed what sort of people they might be. Creoles, they decided, not quite knowing what creoles were. It did not matter. If there were people there was food and water.

But as they advanced they realized that they were not going straight towards the island. Although the float's bow was pointing towards the trees, it was drifting obliquely and would pass a mile or two to port. So they lowered the sail and, using both paddles, tried to drive the float across the wind. This needed a tremendous effort which would have been impossible without the inspiration which they felt. At last, about noon, they calculated that they were directly up wind of the island and hoisted the sail again.

They were only a few miles away from it. But with both sail and paddles they could scarcely manage to come closer.

"The tide is against us," Number Four said.

But they went on paddling as much as they could. As they came closer they began to hear a low, rhythmical roaring sound. The white crescent which guarded the island was explained. The tired swell still had the strength to break with fury on a coral reef.

Thank God the tide was against them! A mile off shore they lowered the sail again and began to paddle round the island looking for an opening in the reef. They soon found one, at the north-eastern corner. There was a calm gap about ten yards wide in the tumbling surf. They hung with their paddles on the tide, waiting for it to change. While they remained stationary, looking over the side, they saw two sharks, one quite ten feet long and another one about six feet long, slowly circling the float a couple of fathoms below the surface.

SEA★WYF

They also saw the island in greater detail. No human beings were to be seen, but any settlement would be on the leeward side. Childhood stories of desert islands came into their minds.

The sun was low above the palm trees when the tide turned. The float, guided by the paddles, began to be sucked towards the reef. The sharks followed it closely, their whiplike bodies slowly undulating, their pale eyes looking upwards with a patient sort of interest. The thunder of surf was now as loud as the cheering of a football crowd. The coral was hidden under the frothing water, but if the float even touched it the rubber would be torn to pieces.

Tired arms tried to guide the craft towards the center of the narrow entrance. It spun out of control. Then on a great heave of the swell which roared deafeningly on either side it was carried through. The sharks were left behind. The float was in calm green water. The paddles touched the sandy bottom.

Biscuit and Bulldog clambered out and tried to walk up the beach, but they felt the island tilting drunkenly, rising and falling like a stormy sea. They collapsed, dizzy, on the sand. Sea-Wyf and Number Four joined them. They lay close together in that seemingly enormous space. They dug their toes and fingers into the sand, trying to embrace the earth. They wept, and sank into a kind of sleep.

They were roused by a rustling, whispering sound and by the consciousness that they were being watched. All around them in the twilight hundreds of eyes were glowing. There was the scarcely audible patter of feet. Sharp, inquisitive noses touched their prostrate bodies. The island was inhabited by rats.

CHAPTER TWENTY

THE island was the shape of a mutton chop. It was about half a mile across at its widest point and altogether two miles long, the termination being a mere sandpit. It was surrounded by a coral reef which was continually awash under frothing breakers on the windward, convex side. This surrounding reef was broken in four places, giving access to a moatlike lagoon where the water was calm and green and shallow. The rim of the island itself was a beach of glistening white sand, generally hot to the touch, and so fine and dry that one's toes sank into it. Inland from the beach was a zone of bushes, something like laurels in appearance. Inland of these on the very gradually rising ground was a zone of feathery trees. On the central and highest part, about thirty feet above sea level, was a grove of coconut palms, tall stately trees forever swaying in the wind, metallically rustling their long sword-like fronds.

Such was their island, but it was some time before the castaways knew it as well as this. At first they slept upon the float, the only place where they felt safe, and when they went ashore they crawled because they lacked the strength to walk more than a few yards at a time.

Biscuit and Bulldog made the first reconnaissance. They looked for water and found none. Crawling, they felt horribly near the rats. There were rats everywhere—heads down, staring with beadlike eyes—rising on their haunches for a better view, sharp, whiskered noses trying to get the scent —scampering forward with sudden rushes to investigate and stopping just out of reach of the weak, clumsily directed blows. "Get away, you little beasts! Get away . . ."

In the palm grove the exhausted men found coconuts which had been eaten out and left as dry as skulls. Then, while they rested back to back, they heard one fall. They scrambled and fell upon it, driving off the rats. It was a lovely thing in its smooth green husk, and when they picked it up they could hear the liquid sloshing about inside it. But they could not get it open.

At last they rolled it back to the float. There Number Four, who had slept all day, cracked it without much difficulty between two lumps of coral rock, disclosing the white lusciousness within. And that night it rained heavily. They were able to supplement their meal with hardtack and then to move to an islet in the lagoon where they were untroubled by rats.

On coconuts they became strong enough to walk. Biscuit and Bulldog collected a dozen more during the first few days, for the wind blew up into another gale. To suck down their throats the cool, vaguely sweet liquid was a consummation of the delights which had so often tantalized them in thirsty dreams. They learned to keep a piece of the white flesh in their mouths, slowly masticating it like chewing gum, gradually extracting the oily nourishment. They could not eat more quickly, or in any quantity, which was no doubt fortunate for their stomachs.

Within a week they were getting about fairly well—Biscuit, Bulldog and Sea-Wyf. Number Four remained on the islet in the lagoon, sleeping most of the time, eating the nuts they brought him and shellfish which he grubbed at low tide, supplemented by a few rats which he killed. To a certain extent the other men resented this complete idleness, but on the whole they were glad that he kept out of the way. He seemed perfectly content so long as Sea-Wyf talked to him now and then, was kind and sympathetic.

So the others explored the island without him. The masts which they had seen belonged to an ancient wooden barque which had driven right across the reef into the lagoon and was there coming to pieces and sinking into the sand.

There were other signs of human habitation. On the leeward side of the island was a corrugated iron shed. Outside it were some wooden frames which presumably had been used for drying coconut flesh to form copra. And close by, screwed to a tall and solitary palm, was an iron box which must once have been painted red.

"Pity they mutilated that," Biscuit said. "It would have been useful for water. We shall need all we can get."

They were still living very much from hand to mouth, but they were cheerful. They had that gratifying sensation of convalescents who find a noticeable improvement in their

strength each day. They moved their quarters to the corrugated shack—all except Number Four who seemed to
prefer his idle, dreamy solitude. The shack was divided
into two rooms, and a lean-to at the back. Though ram-
shackle, it was comfortingly houselike. And it was rat-proof.

It must be stated that the rats were not as numerous as they
had at first appeared. There were thousands of them but they
did not cover the ground, and they had begun to show a
decent, perhaps inherited, respect for humans as soon as these
began to walk upright and to carry sticks.

One day Biscuit came upon a group of rats busy with what
appeared to be a ping-pong ball. But when he had scattered
them nothing remained except a few small pieces of rubbery
shell. Evidently there was another source of food besides
coconuts and the creatures which squirmed at low tide. But
what? The piece of shell was not part of a bird's egg.

The men and the woman kept to their beds at night. These
were only roughly made things of branches, leaves and dried
grass, but after the float they seemed luxurious, and besides,
weak and tired as they still were, they found that they needed
the twelve hours of darkness for rest. But on one occasion,
for the prosaic reason that his insides were out of order,
Biscuit left the hut very early in the morning. Enticed by
the cool half-light he took a walk.

At a spot not far above the high water line he saw a strange
commotion. A large number of little creatures, which at the
distance of a hundred yards he could not recognize, seemed
to be emerging from the sand and making for the sea in a

straggling line. They did not get far unmolested. The whole predatory life of the island swung into action.

Gannets swooped upon the column and made off with victims in their beaks. From high above hovering frigate birds dived upon the gannets, making them disgorge their prey and catching it as it fell. On the ground, rats appeared from everywhere, and charged. But still the little creatures struggled on, those which remained, like brave but untrained soldiers making a dash for it from their dugouts against hopeless odds.

By now Biscuit was on the scene. The attackers were too busy to take notice of him but he picked up one of the attacked. It was like a black button, less than two inches in diameter, but soft as velvet. Flipper-like limbs extended from the button and tried convulsively, even in his hand, to go on waddling. A reptilian head at the end of an elongated neck craned from side to side and almond-shaped myopic eyes stared with desperate anxiety.

He carried it to the sea and put it in. Then he sat down and longed for a cigarette. He was exhausted by the effort of running. When he got to his feet again and looked round, the scene of the carnage had been tidied up as if by magic. The green island in the morning light was beautiful and kindly as paradise. And yet how suddenly this mood could change.

He went to the place from which the baby turtles had appeared and, scraping in the sand, found pieces of eggshell, like bits of ping-pong balls. He and the others had seen adult turtles swimming outside the reef. Vaguely, incuriously they had connected them with the groove-shaped tracks which ran from the high water level up the beach, looking as if a heavy sack had been dragged through the sand. But lacking both a knife and fire for cooking, and still feeling too weak for any violent exertion, they had scarcely wondered when the armored reptiles came ashore. But now the tracks seemed to have a significant and useful meaning.

Biscuit, Bulldog and Sea-Wyf made a night excursion. This resulted in what to them was a wonderful discovery. During the dark hours the female turtles came ashore from the sea where they had played and made love all day. They waddled slowly up the sand. Each female dug hole after hole until finally she was satisfied with one. Then, at the bottom of the hole, she layed a clutch of about two hundred eggs. That done she filled the hole and waddled complacently back to the sea.

Sea-Wyf would not hear of a turtle being killed, but she joined in the collection of eggs. These proved both good and nourishing, not much different in taste from the yolk of hens' eggs.

Growing rapidly stronger, Biscuit, Bulldog and Sea-Wyf began to walk about their island for pleasure. They became fond of their little solitary world. There were shady avenues among the palms and the casuarina trees which fringed the grove. But the greatest beauty lay in the green pools by the shore and among the many tinted corals. There brilliantly colored fishes swam, anemonies waved orange or scarlet tentacles, shellfish gleamed like pearls. Bathing there was like swimming in a pool set with precious stones.

Bright days of sun and wind with the tang of surf in the air, cool moonlit or starlit evenings, nights of sleep and glorious dawns followed each other in procession. The only variation was when it rained, and that was welcome too for then the float which had been placed under the eaves of the shack so that it caught the drip was half filled with water. They were no longer thirsty all the time and could think of other things.

They began to wonder about each other. Bulldog was not communicative. Biscuit had guessed, if he had not been actually told, that he was connected with the law, and he had been given the impression that Bulldog was an important member of it. He asked no questions. Apart from their tacit bond not to do so, he was more interested in Bulldog's present usefulness than in his past. He was intensely curious about Sea-Wyf's history however. Both men were. From her voice and manners she seemed to have the background of a good family. She was evidently well-educated. She could walk gracefully, and swim. She was clever with her hands, weaving mats and baskets. She had an intense appreciation of the beauties of nature. She seemed to love solitude but her companions too. She was soft-hearted yet possessed enough strength of character to make her wishes commands—and this quite apart from her sex, on which she never relied. They knew her qualities well enough, but nothing of her life. She never spoke about herself at all. It was as if she had no past and no future.

But she was a most sympathetic listener to other people's stories. Biscuit told her about himself. He spoke in a manner which he had developed in his school days, boasting of failures. After being rusticated from Oxford—"a nice country-loving touch, don't you think?"—he had taken up a good commercial appointment which his father had obtained for him with a Hong Kong firm. But he "lost that quicker than anybody else could have done," and, left to himself, had developed his theory of success without tears. This consisted of moving down a stratum or two in society to a level where his education and breeding gave him advantage. Thus he had become a steward on a luxury liner, an attendant on a long-distance train, "raking in the tips." When war broke out he was back in the Far East, barman at the smartest hotel in Singapore. By nationality he was Irish and therefore free from the call up. He had considered volunteering in spite of that, but having observed senior officers from the business side of a bar, which is like a keyhole view into the human soul, he had decided that it was all a waste of time. The fall of Singapore had proved that he was right.

Always in the past he had scored a great success with this sort of talk. But with Sea-Wyf, although she was sympathetic and understanding, he found himself feeling ashamed that he had no more genuine achievements to tell her about. For the first time, when there was no scope for ambition, he sincerely wanted to do something worth while.

In the circumstances the best thing he could think of doing was to climb a palm tree. Bulldog made no attempt at this. He said that he could more easily prove by argument that coconuts grew underground than shin up a tree like a nigger. Yet both men felt it desirable that they should collect fruit by some means safe from the rats, for they expected the harvest to end, just as turtles' laying season must soon end.

To master the climbing knack cost Biscuit more determined effort that he had ever before expended in his life. It also cost him most of the skin off the inside of his legs. And when at last he was among the branches and the long waving fronds his sense of achievement was at first drowned in nausea. He was seventy feet above the earth and the slim tree was swaying to and fro. But gradually his vision cleared, and he saw Sea-Wyf, a tiny figure far below, clapping her hands. Bulldog beside her, Biscuit thought, looked more than a little crestfallen.

After that the collection of fruit went rapidly. Sea-Wyf found the leaves useful too, plaiting them to make a dozen different household utensils, hats, and garments. Biscuit was the hero of the hour. But his real triumph came a few days later. It was a particularly clear evening, and from the top of a tree he saw, far away on the horizon, other palms projecting from the water.

So they were not alone in space. That realization added the

sense of security necessary to their lotus-eating life. Biscuit's Island, as they called it, must surely be inhabited, or another visible from it must be inhabited. The chances of eventually being found appeared secure. Yet only as a very last resort did they consider putting to sea again in the float. The memory of their voyage was too vivid. They had nightmares about it still.

So the days passed uncounted, busy yet scarcely eventful, pleasant and satisfying. There were no quarrels. Biscuit and Bulldog were always more or less jealous of each other. But they had the common purpose of collecting food and when their tempers became frayed they could take it out on Number Four. Sea-Wyf was impartially pleasant to all of them. She had healed their sores and now she attended to their daily comfort. Every morning she visited Number Four on his islet. Although the other two men resented this faithful attention to the drone of the party, they accepted it as they had come to accept all that she did. They did not try to understand Number Four. He was either sick or shamming which came to much the same thing. It was a remarkably harmless form for incipient madness to take. That a white woman should wait upon him and sit chatting with him by the hour was all that he could require of life.

"It takes all sorts to make a desert island," Biscuit said.

Their tolerance no doubt largely derived from the fact that they no longer feared the big mulatto. They had seen him making a few tentative expeditions ashore. Sticks were no help to him. He could find none of a shape which he could satisfactorily grip. Besides, they sank deeply into the soft sand. He had to hop, resting on his knee every twenty yards. And when he tripped and fell the rats appeared from hiding. Bulldog who was fitter than he had been for years and Biscuit who could climb palm trees could afford to be magnanimous.

One morning started with a typically domestic scene— the woman looking tired and strained and the men persuading her to spend the day in her bunk.

"You've got a touch of sun, I expect," Bulldog said.

She finally agreed to rest on condition that they carried provisions and her excuses to Number Four.

They said they would, and meant it too. But when they reached the palm grove they left the basket hanging on a tree out of reach of the rats and forgot about it in the athletic excitement of collecting nuts. Towards noon they had their own refreshment, then took the long siesta which had become their habit. It was pleasant under the shade of the palms, on this highest point of the island where they got the breeze. They slept.

They were wakened by Sea-Wyf.

"You shouldn't have come. You don't look at all well," Bulldog said.

"We were just going to take that basket to Number Four," Biscuit added.

She stood in front of them, her closed fingers clasping her thumbs. She looked frightened and she was out of breath.

"We must go from here," she said.

"Where — to the shack?"

"To Biscuit's Island."

"Why do you say that? We have plenty of food."

"We can take the food with us," she said.

"But we have discussed and settled that," Bulldog answered. "You know how difficult the float is to paddle, or to control under sail. Why should we risk our lives? Someone is bound to come here sooner or later."

"So you will not go." She sounded very much disturbed. She turned to Biscuit.

"And you?" she asked.

"I can't see much point in going, I must admit," he answered. "Please tell us what is the matter."

She stood looking at him with dark, troubled eyes. Then she turned away and said almost to herself, "If you will not go with me I must go alone."

CHAPTER TWENTY-ONE

When they returned to the shack they found that Number Four was there. They had guessed as much. But neither then nor at any other time did Sea-Wyf make reference to the incident, whatever it might have been, which had driven her up to the palm grove in such an unusual state of perturbation.

She soon became as calm and self-contained as ever. She saw the argument that if she took the float she would leave her companions stranded, and agreed to stay until they built another craft.

That did not mean that there was not trouble between the men, all the more bitter perhaps because the actual cause was unknown. Sea-Wyf for once did not try to intervene. She merely extracted a promise that there would be no violence and then shut herself in the inner room.

Directly she had gone Bulldog began to lash Number Four with his tongue. Biscuit wondered at his gift for hard words and sharply pointed phrases. Bulldog was going much further, saying far more painful things than he himself would ever have done. He could only sit and listen, with much the same sensations as if he had been watching a flogging, while the mulatto was told that he was the lowest form of life which crawled upon this earth, and that he had only been kept alive by charity of which he could expect no more unless he learned and kept his place. Bulldog stopped short of ordering him back to his islet because he did not know how to enforce the order. But he told him to go and live in the outhouse like the dog he was.

Number Four listened to all this in silence. He had not spoken at all since their return to the shack. At the end of the tirade he rose and hopped to the door. But just before closing it behind him he cast upon his persecutors, and particularly upon Bulldog, a look from his white-rimmed eyes which to men less angry would have been frightening for its malignity.

Bulldog and Biscuit talked plans late into the night—or rather Bulldog, whose blood was up and who was impatient of arguments, stated what these plans should be. Sea-Wyf's wishes apart, he said, they ought to build a really sturdy raft and sail to the other island as soon as possible. It could not be more than one or two days' journey, but to be on the safe side of every possible risk the raft must be big and steady and supplied with enough water and food for a month at least.

Next morning they walked to the wreck, taking Sea-Wyf with them. The barque seemed to offer the likeliest source of materials for building a raft—the only one in fact, for without saws and axes trees could not be used. But the old sailing ship was not at all promising for their purpose. The broken planks of her sides were worm-eaten and for the most part waterlogged. The deck appeared fairly sound, but just for that reason it would be extremely difficult to get it to pieces. As for the masts, much the same problem applied to them as to trees.

"What we need is tools," Bulldog said.

"I never thought of that," Biscuit murmured. It annoyed him that the peace of their Eden had been destroyed and that Bulldog who could not climb palm trees had taken command.

Bulldog ignored the sarcasm. "There must be *something* we can use," he said, and began exploring the wreck, full of energy and determination. The others followed him about.

The wreck had been stripped by storms or human agency of everything easily movable. The rest did not seem much use. For instance, the metal stays were so corroded that the individual wires of which they were made had broken here and there and stood out like rusty thorns. The deck rang hollow under their feet, and below there was only sand and the water of the lagoon with a school of gaily colored fishes swimming inquisitively about among the weed-green plants and ribs.

"I wonder why fish always seem to enjoy a wreck," Biscuit said.

Sea-Wyf smiled and answered, "They feel that they are getting their own back, I expect."

She glanced at Bulldog who evidently was not in the same mood.

"Please forget what I said yesterday," she said to him. "I lost my courage for a little and I am ashamed of it. Naturally we will stay together till the end."

"I trust that we shall—we three," Bulldog answered. "But we need a sturdy raft and the determination to push on. You were quite right to that extent. We were getting into much too much complacent a state of mind. . . .By Jove!"

He was standing in the bow, looking at the anchor. "This will do for getting the deck planks apart," he said.

"How would we put them together again?" Biscuit asked.

Before Bulldog could answer, Sea-Wyf said, "Why take the deck to pieces? Why not use it whole?"

That, more or less, is what they did. During the following days the old bulwarks creaked and yielded under the blows of the anchor which, working together, the two men wielded like a sledge hammer or crowbar. Gradually the deck was prized up. In several large pieces they tipped it into the lagoon.

But it was a bitter disappointment when they saw how low the hardwood floated. It was awash and would support no weight. They needed far more buoyancy. That meant that they must use the masts.

Before beginning the tremendous task of unshipping these they took the deck round to the leeward side of the island. They accomplished this by pulling and pushing it, wading and swimming in the lagoon.

In the middle of this operation Bulldog went ahead to select a beaching site. Biscuit and Sea-Wyf rested, up to their waists in the warm water, their hands on the floating deck, tiny fish playing about their toes. Biscuit felt cheerful as a boy, but Sea-Wyf was gazing in the direction of the shack, and her profile, which was all he could see, looked serious and troubled.

He said on an impulse, "Don't worry about Number Four. Your spell will hold."

She faced him, "You know my thoughts?"

"I often seem to—. But please don't look so startled. It's a great bond."

She smiled. He had noticed it before but now it struck him particularly, how her serious face lit up when she smiled. She was wearing a big hat which she had woven out of palm fronds. It made a green halo round her head. Her neck and shoulders glowed golden in the sun. Biscuit felt a sudden heat inside him, then the prickling emptiness of longing.

"Sea-Wyf," he said.

She did not answer but, holding his eyes, a deeper color mounted from her neck into her face.

"It's quite all right," he said. "I know the rules although you have not spoken them. I promise not to make things more difficult for you than they are. But when we get somewhere safe, when this is all over—"

"Then you will do something worth while," she said.

"Yes, I will. But you—how will you feel? Will you—? Please give me something to hold onto. If you do I promise never to speak of this again until we are safe."

The color had gone from her face. Standing in the water, in her ragged garment, she looked forlorn.

"When we are safe," he repeated, not knowing what his lips said, speaking with his eyes.

She very slightly shook her head.

"Then we must say good-by," she answered.

"I'll leave you alone for as long as you want, until we have fitted into life again. But I'll be waiting. I would know if you died, I'm certain I would know if anything happened to you or if you needed me. There is a bond, isn't there?"

She nodded.

"Then you do feel—?"

"It does not matter what I feel," she said in a flat voice.

"Matter? Of course it matters. That is the one important thing."

He started to move towards her through the water. He wanted to touch her, to take her in his arms. But her expression halted him.

"Do you believe—?" she began, and stopped. She closed her eyes for a moment, then opened them again and said, looking straight at him, "The one important thing now, is that we should stay together, all four of us, working together, struggling for the same thing, trusting in God. But directly we are safe Biscuit and Sea-Wyf, Bulldog and Number Four will cease to exist. They will have other names, go different ways. I have spoken with Bulldog of this and he agrees completely."

"He would! He thinks only of himself. He does not want

when we are safely home to have any of us hanging around him intimately, making claims of friendship. But I only think of you, and will not hide behind a nickname. I'm Michael Cannan, of no fixed address but the Garrick Club would find me. Will you not repay the confidence and tell me who you are?"

He stood close beside her in the water, waiting for her reply.

Bulldog's voice came to them.

"Sea-Wyf, Biscuit. Come along!"

She started and half smiled.

"That is who we are," she said. "Sea-Wyf and Biscuit who must build a raft."

There were still nuts to be collected. Biscuit, who took a pride in his skill, selected the young fruit which was full of milk and comparatively easily opened. They all took turns in the search for turtles' eggs. Number Four, who from a solitary mystic had been forced into the position of a sort of house boy did what he was told to do, living in a mood of grimly patient silence, appearing still more lonely than he had been when he was by himself. But he was useful. In a series of channels and dammed pools made at low tide he trapped a number of fish. He slit them open with a broken shell, salted them with brine and hung them up to cure in wind and sun.

The others spent most of their working hours in the construction of the raft. Their ambitions had grown. It was not only going to be a sturdy raft. It was going to be the biggest and best in the whole history of castaways. They used to talk about it in the evenings. Number Four listened and often seemed upon the point of joining in. In some ways they would have welcomed his advice, for after all he was a sailor. But they excluded him from having anything to do with their raft. He had to be kept in his place.

By tremendous efforts, knocking the whole wreck more or less to pieces, they managed to unship the masts. They floated them round to the place opposite a break in the reef where the decking had been beached. There, on a level which they calculated would be under water at the next full moon tide, they put the raft together.

It was enormous, most imposing. But the pieces were not securely joined. Such nails and screws as they had been able to salvage were hard to use effectively. Lashings would have been better. But their attempts to make rope were not successful. Biscuit thought that the anchor chain might do, until Bulldog pointed out that it would slip unless they could cut notches in the wood.

"One misses fire for cooking," he said. "But we have never needed it as much as now. With fire we could forge tools."

They thought of the various ways in which they had tried to make fire, and failed. They suffered from heat but could not make a flame.

"I asked Number Four if he couldn't do it native fashion, rubbing two sticks together," Bulldog went on. "And d'you know what he said? He said he didn't know nothing about that sort of thing because he was an edicated man."

"Yet I believe he might help us if you encouraged him a little," Sea-Wyf said.

"Encourage him! The only chance with a fellow like that is to keep him under. I know the type."

And Biscuit felt as hardly towards the mulatto as Bulldog did, for Sea-Wyf had promised Number Four that she would be kind to him when they reached safety while to himself she had offered nothing except a good-by. He wondered jealously what there could be between those two, what they had talked about during their long conversations on the islet.

One evening, a week before the full moon tide, they were returning to the shack, pleasantly tired, looking forward to their simple meal before the light went, then to sleep. They saw Number Four squatting outside, and wondered what he was doing so busily. His two hands were held together and he was working them up and down with a pumping action just above the sand. Then he raised an arm and something in his hand glittered like a mirror in the sun. Next moment he saw them approaching. He lowered his arm and sat waiting. He was holding a knife with a broad blade more than a foot in length.

"What have you got there?" Bulldog shouted.

"A machete," Number Four grinned.

"Where the devil did you find it?"

"Smoothing the sand in the shed. Lots of things buried

there. It was black. But see now." He picked up a pencil stub and sharpened it as neatly as if he had been using a penknife. "Good steel don't grow old."

"Let's have a look at it," Bulldog said, holding out his hand.

The cunning, self-satisfied look which they had not seen for so long spread over the mulatto's face. His eyes glinted.

"No. You got most things I haven't got, but I got this," he began again to polish the blade in the sand.

Sea-Wyf looked meaningly at her two companions and made a slight gesture with her hands. They understood her, but hestitated. She repeated the gesture and they moved unwillingly away. From beyond earshot they saw the girl sit down beside Number Four, saw them talking together for some time. At last she rose and walked slowly up to Bulldog and Biscuit.

"He would not give it to me," she said. "But he has promised not to use it for—for anything wrong."

Bulldog stared, then broke out, "And must we stake our lives on the word of a—"

"Yes," Sea-Wyf said. "You must do that. I can do no more. *You* need not be afraid."

CHAPTER TWENTY-TWO

Number Four did not actually threaten them, either in words or action. If he had, Bulldog and Biscuit in spite of Sea-Wyf's entreaties would have taken the risk of attacking him. On the contrary, he was jovial. As Biscuit cynically said, he was frightfully decent about everything. He laughed a great deal. He seemed to be enjoying an endlessly amusing private joke. He treated them all with the greatest familiarity. But always, night and day, the long sharp blade was either in his hand or slung in its sheath at his hip, hanging where his other leg should have been. It was like a symbol of authority.

He became as energetic as his one leg allowed. "You think you can build a raft. Now I show you," he said. And he did. He notched the masts neatly and deeply so that the chain fitted securely into place as it spiraled round the three long poles and over the decking. The two longer masts were placed lengthwise on the outside, the shorter between them, leaving parallel gaps three feet wide. These gaps were wedged with some vertically placed planks to act as leeboards. Over this lower layer, which formed the main bulk, was placed the decking. The two layers were kept together principally by a chain. But Number Four showed that, when he wanted to, he could make quite an efficient rope from grasses and creepers. This he used for a hundred well-tied lashings and—at Sea-Wyf's request—for safety ropes which were looped along the sides. To the deck were tied a number of baskets and similar contraptions which were to be used as beds and for storing supplies. The rubber float was secured in the center as a water tank. There was also a three-legged mast and a square sail, something like the sail of a Chinese junk, woven from palm fronds.

When the raft was completed they were all proud of it.

"You're a clever fellow, Number Four, I must grant you that," Bulldog said.

"I'm clever all right, all right," the mulatto answered, grinning. "But I ain't Number Four no longer. I'm the Captain. You call me Captain."

Biscuit looked at Bulldog, waiting for an angry reply. But Bulldog answered, "Yes, you have earned that title, Captain."

While waiting for the full moon tide they got their stores together—baskets of coconuts and turtles eggs, hampers of dried fish. There was enough for a couple of months—they were taking no chances. Lastly—called for by Number Four and collected by Biscuit—there was a bunch of crown shoots from the high tops of half a dozen trees, the succulent palmiste which is eaten only as the rarest luxury because the whole tree dies when it is picked.

"This very good. This for the big moment," Number Four said, grinning.

He was excited, teeth and eyes gleaming in his dusky face. They did not ask what he meant by the big moment.

The spring high tide, they had calculated, was due at one hour before sunset on the day of the full moon. They waited for it anxiously, for the previous tide had not quite floated the raft and it was too late to think of getting rollers under that enormous mass of wood.

There were no waves in the lagoon. The water advanced very slowly, like a stain, wetting the hot dry sand. The bow end of the raft began to float. Gradually the huge, clumsy concoction of logs and planks came to life. The three men and the woman threw their shoulders against the levers which they had placed under the stern. For an agonizing minute they strained without effect. Very slowly at first, then smoothly and fast the raft slid forward and rode upon the water.

They raised a cheer and plunged in after it. They scrambled on board.

When they were all on the same side the raft began slowly and majestically to tilt. They laughed, and walked to the other side to correct the movement. They could walk on it—it was as big as that. Fore and aft it was absolutely steady whatever they did. It gave them a wonderful sense of confidence. They anchored it and began to load the stores.

By the time that they had finished it was night—not dark

because of the moon. Number Four announced that they would start at dawn, with the next ebb. Several of the lashings needed readjustment.

"You help me, Bulldog?"

Bulldog, in his strangely acquiescent mood, agreed.

Biscuit and Sea-Wyf stood on the shore.

"I need a few more fronds for the sail," the girl said. "And don't you think it would be nice to leave some food in the shack in case anybody else comes to the island as we did. Will you gather some more coconuts?"

"If you come with me," Biscuit said.

Immediately afterwards he regretted saying that. The island in the full moonlight had an unearthly loveliness—the mother-of-pearl shades of sand and water, the tall stately trees, the mysterious rustle of their fronds and solemn boom of surf. It was almost more than flesh and blood could stand to be so close to this girl and not to take her in his arms. Yet, somehow, the same strong power which bound him to her prevented him from touching her.

It was a relief to climb a tree. To be so high on such a night brought a thrill of exaltation. He lingered over his work, drinking in the beauty and the peace.

A movement caught his eye. Someone was swimming from the raft to the shore. A tall figure emerged and began hopping along the sea border, grotesque in the moonlight. A minute or two later Bulldog also landed and followed him, running. Biscuit wondered what they were up to, but

only vaguely, disinterestedly. He climbed down and joined
Sea-Wyf. They gathered up the nuts and palm fronds and
walked silently to the shack.

Voices approached them. Number Four's angrily raised,
Bulldog's answering flatly, dogmatically. Even when the
men reached the shack it was difficult to understand at first
exactly what had happened. Apparently, while they were
working on the raft, Number Four had caught sight of a
turtle making for the sea. He had at once dived overboard
in an attempt to intercept it. But Bulldog followed too
slowly and the creature had escaped. That was not all, for
when they returned to the raft the machete could not be
found. Number Four said that he had left it on the deck,
Bulldog that he had not noticed it before he followed. For
half an hour they had searched through the paraphernalia
on deck and Number Four had made repeated dives to the
clear sandy bottom of the lagoon. He was certain that it
had not fallen overboard.

"It must be on deck. We'll find it in the morning," Bulldog said.

"In any case," Sea-Wyf said, "the knife has served its
purpose. We do not need it any more."

"Need it? Sure I need it," Number Four fumbled with
the empty sheath.

"I dare say we will find it," Sea-Wyf said.

"If you find it you give it to me?"

"Yes."

"You make the others give it me?"

"Yes. Let us go to bed now. We must start early with the tide."

Biscuit could not sleep. He lay turning and shifting on his bed. He was impatient to start the voyage. He was impatient to end it, to prove himself in life for Sea-Wyf's sake.

He rose and went out. He judged that it must be almost dawn and walked down to the shore. The wind, a mild but steady breeze, was blowing in the right direction. Conditions were ideal. He waited until the sun broke surface and the palms threw out their barlike shadows across the sea. Then he went back to wake the others.

Sea-Wyf came out and started for the beach with the rolled sail under her arm. Bulldog followed her.

"You ready?" Number Four shouted from his shed.

"Just going to have another look for your machete and tidy up the deck," Bulldog answered. "We'll have everything shipshape by the time you get aboard, Captain."

"That's right. That's right." There was a laugh. Number Four seemed to be enjoying his endlessly funny private joke.

Bulldog jerked Biscuit by the arm. "Hurry," he whispered. They ran, took Sea-Wyf by the hand and ran on. They plunged into the lagoon, waded and swam to the raft. They climbed aboard, panting.

Bulldog at once cast loose. He took up one of the float paddles and handed the other to Biscuit.

"What are you doing? What about Number Four?" Sea-Wyf asked.

"He's just coming. It will take a bit of time maneuvering to the gap," Bulldog answered.

They paddled hard. The big raft began gradually to move. It was not easy to turn it so that it would pass cleanly through the gap to the open sea. The tide was sucking out, tending to pull it against the coral. But, working hard, Biscuit understanding although he had not been told, they got the raft into the full current, and then all they had to do was to keep it moving straight.

"There he is, coming down. We must not go any farther," Sea-Wyf said.

Bulldog ignored her. "Now the sail. Quick," he said.

"No! You mean to leave him behind," Sea-Wyf faced him.

"Of course I'm leaving him behind. Give me the sail."

"No. You shall not leave him to starve."

Bulldog stood in front of her. If he tried to snatch the sail from her it would tear.

"I am not leaving him behind to starve. Those coconuts —and there are plenty of rats."

"You are a coward," she said.

"I am not. I am the only one with a clear brain and the courage to use it. You know what would happen if he came on board. And I am not leaving him to die. As soon as we find help we can send back for him. Give me the sail."

"No. It is deceitful, unfair."

Number Four had reached the water's edge, but the raft, carried by the ebb, was a hundred yards out. Bulldog stood judging the distance.

"All right, we must paddle," he said. "Help me, Biscuit."

"Biscuit!" Sea-Wyf said.

"But Bulldog is right, you know."

"Biscuit, please!"

"For God's sake let us have reason, not sentiment," Bulldog burst out. "If he comes on board it's a hundred to one he will cause trouble. You know that as well as I do. If we sail out of reach he will turn back, and we can send to collect him, probably in a few days. Which is the right thing to do? I ask you in the name of reason—you who were so frightened by him that you were prepared to sail away alone."

"Very well," Sea-Wyf said unhappily. "Call to him to turn back. Tell him that we will send to fetch him."

The two men shouted and waved. But Number Four, ploughing through the water, could not or would not understand.

Bulldog waved his paddle. "You fool, I'll make you understand with this. Go back. You are not wanted here."

"Look!" Sea-Wyf said breathlessly.

Between the swimmer and the shore a triangular fin was cutting the water.

"I don't care," Bulldog shouted in a fury. "That's his look out. Go back, you fool." He waved the paddle.

"Stop him, Biscuit."

Biscuit laid his hand on Bulldog's arm. With the shark nosing cautiously behind his splashing foot Number Four reached the float. He rested his elbows on the side.

"You let me come on board? Very kind!" He grinned.

Then with a thrust of his leg and a heave of his muscular body he was on the raft.

At dawn next morning they saw Biscuit's Island, only a few miles away, almost directly downwind. From its formation and vegetation it might have been the island they had left and this similarity unreasonably disturbed them.

But they were impatient to arrive. It was taken for granted they would land even if they saw no signs of habitation. They had had quite enough of this raft voyage already. It had not been pleasant with Number Four continually rummaging about in search of his machete. And they disliked the raft itself. It was so sluggish and cumbersome. In spite of its size they felt as if they were actually in the ocean—a quite different sensation from skimming over it in the float. And because of its size it was difficult to steer. It took several minutes of hard paddling to change direction by even a few degrees, and then the bows generally swung beyond the point desired. With a pompous solemnity the great logs dipped and rose. The wind had freshened and every wave washed over the unprotected deck.

As they advanced they heard the thunder of the surf, and saw it leaping, savage and frothing, like an endless avalanche. They could distinguish no break in the reef, so, paddling hard, they turned the raft to make it pass along the side of the island.

Moving slowly in spite of the fresh wind they traveled the length of the island, half a mile from the reef. Still there was no gap. The waves, sweeping obliquely over the coral, looked murderous as before.

They lowered the sail and began to turn across the wind making for the lee of the island. As soon as the raft came round it started to roll, and the waves swept right over it from side to side. Paddling under these conditions was difficult and dangerous, but they kept the bow heading for the calmer water. They kept the raft pointing in the right direction, but it was carried sideways by wind and current farther and farther away.

Exhausted and desperate they began shouting at each-other. Should they abandon the raft and launch the float? It would be almost impossible under such conditions, and at best it would mean leaving the stores. No one took the initiative. It was easier to go on paddling—across the wind and finally against it, backwards. At last they gave up trying. They felt utterly helpless aboard the monster they had made.

For the remainder of the day they sat watching the island gradually sinking below the horizon—first the beach, then the bushes and finally the tops of the trees.

After sunset they slept from sheer exhaustion.

At some time during the night Biscuit woke with a start.

He saw Sea-Wyf on her knees, her eyes searching over the moonlit waters.

"What is it?" he whispered.

"I heard a strange sound," she said.

"What sort of sound?"

"I cannot describe it. I was asleep. It woke me up."

Their whispering voices, the heaving water, opal and shadowed, the strange movements of the raft increased the sense of helplessness and fear of the unknown. They stared about them anxiously.

They saw a large black shape rise gradually above the surface, pointing upwards at a steep angle.

"Submarine!" Biscuit shouted.

The others were awake in a moment, staring. More of the black mass became visible. It tilted forward until it was lying horizontally, three-quarters submerged. The front part sank and up came the flat tail, up and up until it was nearly vertical. Then the tail slapped down with the noise of an explosion, and the monster disappeared.

It was a whale. They had realized that before it dived. But as the physical effects of a fright remain after the danger is past, so their minds retained the impression they had received when Biscuit had shouted, "Submarine." The voyage on the float was being repeated like a bad dream.

That was the impression which they all had so strongly that soon they could not prevent themselves from speaking of it. It had started when Number Four had come over the side using, whether consciously or not, the same words as when he had boarded the float. The island had gone down below the horizon like a ship which passed unheeding. A few days later there was a heavy fall of rain—that was the electric storm. Fish gathered under the raft—and they waited for the sharks. They had no actual attack by sharks, but often in the night they saw the phosphorescent lines which they or other hunting creatures drew upon the surface.

Discomforts and irritations which they had half forgotten increased the nightmare sense of repetition. They felt the nervous restlessness which comes from constriction. It became intolerable to remain in the same position, and they disturbed each other by moving about. Although they had plenty to eat and drink each watched jealously how much the others took. And their physical condition rapidly deteriorated. In spite of the hats and matlike garments they had made, the sun burned them cruelly. This must largely have been because they were so frequently soaked by spray. But in any case hardship is more difficult to bear a second time.

The raft lurched and rolled onwards, going very slowly towards nothing.

At the end of the first week the wind freshened.

"Now we get the storm," Number Four announced.

"And reach an island when it is over," Sea-Wyf said smiling.

"Maybe. But this time I reckon something bad's going to happen."

"I am certain it is not," Sea-Wyf said.

"Sure there is. Last night I dreamed of getting married."

"That *is* bad luck," Biscuit laughed.

"Sure it is," Number Four answered with deadly seriousness. "My mother told me that, and it's proved true. She'd dreamed of marriage just before my father swam ashore."

"That dream came true."

"Course not. But there were bad things all right all right with the police looking for him. Only good thing come of that, Mother said, was that I won't die by drowning."

"I'm sure that is right," Bulldog said. "It is written that you will die another way."

"What d'you mean?" Number Four demanded, made suddenly suspicious by the tone.

"He means that he agrees with your mother," Sea-Wyf said.

The rising wind cut short this conversation.

The storm swept up the sea like a vast invisible broom violently handled. The wind was fierce but short-lived. Next morning it dropped suddenly and completely.

But the waves did not go down. They only changed character. A patch of water would suddenly rise straight into the air, forming a cone, then subside upon itself, leaving a frothing hollow. This sort of thing went on all round the raft, often so close that it was tilted at a steep angle or showered with spray. The crew clung on for their lives. But they were not desperate, for they felt sure this must be the death throes of the storm. The sea would go down and then the island would appear.

Up and up went one side of the raft, up and up as it often had before. The crew clung on. Biscuit had found a good place to grip, where the two ends of the chain were bound together with rope. He could hold on there without hurting his hands. The deck cargo slithered and was stopped by the lashings. Water sloshed out of the float.

The raft splashed flat. Half a minute later the other side rose suddenly as a cone of water formed under it. It rose up until the raft was on edge. The raft remained like that for a moment or two, then it splashed flat—upside down.

CHAPTER TWENTY-THREE

Biscuit was underneath, bumping his head against the thing he had been lying on. He did not know which way to swim and he breathed water until he reached the surface. There he clung onto a life line, and the edge of the raft came up and hit him under the chin. He bit his tongue and the pain revived him. He scrambled on board—if the underside of a craft can be described as on board.

He saw Bulldog's legs projecting from under the raft. He caught hold of them and after extraordinary efforts dragged him on board. The other two had been flung clear. Their heads were bobbing in and out of the moving water. Conventional swimming was no use, even for an expert like Number Four, for nothing was horizontal. They splashed about like drowing puppies until the will to survive or Providence or something got them, by the hair or under the armpits, and helped them out.

For a long time they lay embracing the spars or what had been the leeboards while the salt water they had swallowed and inhaled dribbled from their mouths.

The fagots which wedged the mast logs apart were less thick than the solid wood, so they formed two parallel grooves. In these the men and woman lay, in pairs head to feet. Aft lay Biscuit and Number Four, forward of them Sea-Wyf and Bulldog. Sea-Wyf kept an arm over Bulldog while Biscuit held his feet, for he was unconscious. He must have received a blow on the head.

After a little while the three who were undamaged raised their heads. The sea was still rocketing up and down, and it was seething with life. Hundreds of fish were after the stores and sharks were after the fish. There could have been no question of salvaging anything even had the sea allowed it.

Soon it began to blow again, and the waves which had been individually jumping about like Russian dancers fell into ranks and began to march forward with spray flying from their crests. It blew hard for several hours, but the raft, perhaps because of the heavy hardwood deck and the trailing paraphernalia which were now underneath, took comparatively little notice. It wallowed. It was constantly swamped but showed no inclination to turn over again.

This time when the wind eased it did so gradually, so the waves remained ordered until they died down. By the second morning after the beginning of the storm it was calm.

Number Four was the first to sit up. Biscuit, in a mood of sleepy convalescence, watched him as he crawled about exploring. Suddenly the mulatto gave a grunt of surprise and dragged himself towards something which was just projecting from one of the fagots. It was the handle of the machete and he drew out the blade.

That made Biscuit sit up. But Number Four did no more

at first than squat with a worried expression on his face
while he tried to get the new rust off the blade with his fin-
gernails and by rubbing it against the woodwork of the raft.

Biscuit, whose reactions had been slowed to almost the
same extent, sat watching him.

Every now and then Number Four held up the blade to
the sun to see if the glitter were returning to it. Sea-Wyf
noticed him doing this. She drew herself into a sitting position. She was a pathetic sight, her hair and face plastered
with white salt. Bulldog lay without moving, breathing
stertorously. Sea-Wyf watched Number Four for a little
while, then leaning over the side she scooped up some water and began bathing Bulldog's head.

Number Four crawled forward and prodded Bulldog
with the hilt of the machete.

"Leave him alone," Sea-Wyf said. "He is ill."

"I want to know how this got there," Number Four
pointed with the knife.

"It may have slipped down."

"No. No it didn't. It was pushed in."

"It does not matter in any case," Sea-Wyf said. "You
might as well throw the thing away. It isn't any more use."

"Sure it's useful. I show you soon. We'll be all right, you
and me."

"We will all four be all right," Sea-Wyf said.

Number Four looked at her knowingly and nodded.

Sea-Wyf gave a dry cough and tried to swallow.

"Perhaps there is something left under the raft," she

said to him. "Something to eat or drink. Will you look,
please?"

"You want me to go see?"

"Yes, please."

Number Four nodded and smiled. Then he looked troubled. He began to put the machete into the sheath which was
still at his hip. He drew it out again.

"Don't want to spoil this."

"I'll hold it for you if you like," Sea-Wyf said.

"You give it back?"

"Yes—or I'll keep it for you."

"Fine."

Number Four took a number of deep breaths, then he
slipped head first over the side.

Bulldog would have seized the weapon from the girl or
insisted upon its being thrown away, Biscuit thought. But
he himself did nothing except watch her, fascinated. With
the long knife in her hand she looked like a figure of justice—a pathetic and bedraggled figure of justice.

Number Four came up with a grin on his face and a small
coconut in each hand. He handed the nuts on board, and
after a short rest dived again. Altogether he salvaged a dozen
which had been caught up in a basket. There was no sign
of any of the other stores, he said. The rest of the nuts must
have floated away and the eggs and dried fillets been eaten
by fish.

When Number Four came on board again Sea-Wyf
handed the machete to him, and he slit the tops off three of

the nuts, cleanly and expertly, leaving a small hole in the white flesh to fit the lips. When he gave one to the girl she raised Bulldog's head and put it to his mouth.

"Why you do that?"

"He needs it most."

"It's wasted. He's going to die."

Bulldog's eyes blinked open. He looked somberly at Number Four, moved his lips experimentally, then slowly said, "I shall stay alive longer than you."

He closed his eyes again and Sea-Wyf laid his head upon her lap so that her body shaded it from the sun.

"I would like a nut now, please," she said.

They sat drinking the milk of coconuts and talking now and then, strangely perhaps but in quite pleasant tones. They were in a desperate position, God knew where. Their world had been turned upside down. And the atmosphere was like a tea party—never mind if it was a Mad Hatter's tea party. It was the girl's doing, keeping them so calm, Biscuit thought. She was a marvel.

The breeze fell gradually away and was succeeded by a dead calm. Dead is the most appropriate adjective, for after the first two or three days of calm the ocean appeared to be literally without life. It was oily and flat, and there was a smell about it very different from that sensed when a breeze was blowing.

Bulldog had recovered from the direct effects of his concussion, but he was weak. For that matter they all seemed to be weakening rapidly. The storm they had been through must have taken a lot out of them. And there was the disappointment of not finding an island. They felt dispirited and helpless. They sat or lay about, making their ration of three coconuts each last as long as possible, and scarcely talking at all.

Number Four tried to alter the positions which they occupied, though in a different manner from that on the first voyage. Being the fittest of them he had made several more salvage dives. He had brought up some empty baskets which, flattened out, could be used either for bedding or shelter. He made up a sort of couch and invited Sea-Wyf to move to the place beside him.

She refused.

He looked surprised and asked why not.

"We will stay as we are," she said. "But you can share those baskets with the others."

"No. No I don't share," he answered, suddenly furious. "And I don't give nothing to you. You always promise and you do nothing. Bad as the rest."

After that he spent most of the time squatting with his back to them all, staring out over the oily sea.

It may have been two days after this—time was hard to measure—when the others saw his body suddenly stiffen. He leaned forward excitedly. Next moment he slipped over the side without a splash.

He began to swim, not with his usual crawl, but with a careful breast stroke which scarcely ruffled the water.

The others saw what he was making for. A hundred yards away a turtle was lying on the surface, apparently dead.

Number Four approached it from behind. While still some distance away he sank like a seal. For half a minute nothing happened. Then there was a flurry and the turtle was on its back. Number Four's head broke surface, and he began carefully to push the inverted creature towards the raft. It was very much alive, its flippers frantically waving in the air.

"Pull him up. Mind he don't bite."

Biscuit obeyed automatically.

"Keep him on his back."

The turtle lay upside down on the raft, working its flippers desperately and ineffectively. Its leathery neck stretched out. Its mouth opened and closed.

"Sleeping," said Number Four. "I came up underneath like this." He raised his arms, crossed, above his head. "I grip his back flippers. Then—" With a sudden jerk he swung his hands in a half circle. "Pretty neat, eh?"

The turtle gulped. From one of its inverted eyes a sticky tear escaped.

"Why did you catch the poor thing? It is no good to us," Sea-Wyf said.

"No good? Damn good. You wait."

Number Four dragged the turtle to his own section of the raft. He had his back to the others. He drew the machete, which had not been out of his possession since his disagreement with Sea-Wyf. There were several blows. Then the dark shoulders heaved, and there were grunting sounds of effort.

Number Four swung round.

"Look!"

The turtle had been dismembered and lay slit horizontally in half. The limbs and the flattish lower shell were in one place, the basin-like upper shell in another, full of blood and still moving intestines. The mulatto was splashed with blood all over. He crouched, grinning, with the red knife in his hand.

Bulldog whispered angrily to Biscuit, "Why did you let him come on board?"

CHAPTER TWENTY-FOUR

THE hot dead calm broke in a thunderstorm. They got quite a lot to drink while it lasted, and they filled the turtle shell almost to the brim. Of the eatable parts of the creature all which remained were two of the limbs and several dozen eggs, for it had been a female. Biscuit and Bulldog had eaten some of the meat from the limbs, and found it not unlike beef. Sea-Wyf at first had refused to touch anything at all, but at last, being persuaded by Biscuit that it was her duty to look after herself so that she could look after them, had accepted some of the eggs. Number Four had taken his fill from the other parts indiscriminately, and the other parts constituted by far the greater proportion of the carcass.

This feasting went to his head. He retold a score of times the story of how he had turned the turtle. And he demonstrated with the machete how he had butchered the creature, cutting round the leathery body. He spoke of himself as the Captain. He was affable in the same sort of way that he had been on the island after the finding of the knife. The men found not only his manner but also his presence offensive, for if the blood had gone to his head like wine it had gone to his stomach like medicine. And it must have been far worse for Sea-Wyf. Although Number Four did not repeat his invitation that she should share the mats with him, he was forever directing at her meaning glances which she, sometimes evidently, found it difficult to ignore.

Since they had no way of controlling the raft they did not keep watches in the ordinary sense. But one or another of them was always occupied in holding the turtle shell, for otherwise the water would have spilled. It was particularly irksome to be wakened in the night—it always seemed too soon—and have to nurse the precious chalice for an estimated period of two hours. Besides the necessity of keeping still there was the almost intolerable temptation to drink. Unquestionably, this was an additional cause of strain and friction.

One morning Bulldog said that the shell was less full than it had been at nightfall. Their ration was measured with a half coconut shell and handed out at sunset, so none should have gone during the night. They all denied having spilled any.

"Then it has been drunk," Bulldog said.

No one answered, but no doubt the remark was remembered by them all throughout the long heat of the day.

In the evening Bulldog gave some of his own ration to Sea-Wyf and Biscuit.

Next morning they all looked very carefully at what remained of the water in the shell. Nothing was said. But at sunset Bulldog made the same offer as on the previous evening.

Sea-Wyf refused.

"You are still having headaches. You need it more than any of us," she said.

Headaches must be the explanation, Biscuit thought. He wished he could have brought himself to give some of his precious ration to Sea-Wyf. But he could not. The utmost he could do was to refuse any extra.

Number Four sat gloomily watching.

"You going to give some to the Captain?" he asked.

"I think you have had enough," Bulldog answered.

"Enough? I'm biggest."

"You manage very well," Bulldog said.

Number Four considered this. Suddenly he shouted, "You think I stole water?"

"I never said so," Bulldog answered. "You are accusing yourself."

"Nobody accuses anybody," Sea-Wyf said. She was holding the turtle shell in her hands and her face was drawn with anxiety.

Number Four and Bulldog took no notice of her. They sat facing each other a couple of yards apart.

It was not dark although the sun had set, for the whole ocean glowed with phosphorescence. No waves broke except those which struck the raft, but here they seemed to burst into many-colored flames.

"You never said it but you meant it," Number Four's

voice rose—not to a shout but in a series of rasping croaks. "You're afraid of me. You do things behind my back. You never touched the machete, eh? You hid it under the raft. You wanted to sail on and leave me when I swam for the paddle. I saw you. You've been against me all along. But I'm clever."

"For God's sake be quiet. Your voice jars," Bulldog said. His own voice was as harsh as a saw cutting a dry bone.

"You'll not get the better of me. I know who you are. I know how to break you. If I have to wait twenty years—"

Sea-Wyf leaned towards Biscuit.

"Stop them. I can't," she whispered.

She had appealed to him. Since the island—before that—he had wanted to do something noteworthy for her sake. He had pictured himself saving her from a shark—that sort of thing. What could he do now? Those two were quarreling like bad-tempered children, and Number Four had drawn the machete. After all they had been through they were going to be cut to pieces because Bulldog had a headache. Typical of life! He cleared his throat.

"If you want to know who took the water it was me," he said as loudly as he could.

The other two men stopped talking at once and turned on him.

"At least I spilled it," he added. "Do what you like to-morrow, but now let's get some sleep."

They were all sitting bolt upright, their faces lighted by

the extraordinary glow from the sea. And they were all working their lips and swallowing.

Number Four gave a triumphant laugh.

"Sure, let's sleep. I didn't start the trouble." He said it to the girl.

Gradually they relaxed. The men lay down. Sea-Wyf remained upright, holding the shell of water in her lap. She was motionless and statuesque—like a figure on a fountain, Biscuit thought, a fountain illuminated by fairy lights. The phosphorescent glow had increased. The ocean was a vast bowlful of molten stars—lovely with an awe-inspiring loveliness. The only sound was of little waves which chattered against the raft, throwing up tongues of flame.

Cautiously Biscuit raised his head. Both the other men were lying in positions which would allow them to watch the girl. It was impossible to be certain that Bulldog's eyes were open, but those of Number Four glowed like pearls. He seemed peaceful enough, however. Biscuit thought, we shall be all right if they will only relax, go to sleep—it's this extraordinary night.

He lowered his head again. Sea-Wyf had remained absolutely still, the focal point of the lambently glowing world. Above the clear sky seemed black. Under this somber covering the raft with the starved and nerve-wracked people on it floated in flames.

"My turn now!" Number Four suddenly said.

Biscuit and Bulldog were sitting up stiffly in a moment.

"My turn to watch the water."

He reached out his arms towards Sea-Wyf, still holding the knife. She passed the shell to him. As he took it
from her she drew her breath in quickly and flicked her
fingers.

"What's wrong?" Number Four asked.

"You cut me. Please put that thing away."

Balancing the shell in one hand he replaced the machete
in the sheath at his hip. Then he extended his free arm, saying, "Let me see."

He took her hand, pulling her off balance so that she
fell on her knees. He examined the bleeding finger then
put it to his lips.

"Now I have drunk your blood," he said softly.

"Be careful with the water," Sea-Wyf said.

Slowly they composed themselves again. Now the big
dark torso and the black head were the focus of the glow.

Two hours—how could one judge two hours? The stars
had shrunk and faded. Number Four was harmless while
he held the shell. But waiting was intolerable. Biscuit had
almost decided to claim his turn when, without a word,
Number Four handed him the water.

Again they composed themselves, for they had all started
up even at this slight movement.

Biscuit sat with the shell in his hands and the three prone
forms beside him. The phosphorescent light had increased
so much that he could see them all clearly. But how weird
they seemed in that multicolored glow.

There was a movement beside him. Number Four was

crawling towards Sea-Wyf with the strange lopsided action of a wounded animal.

Biscuit placed the shell on the deck but still supported it with his hands. He saw Bulldog stiffen. He saw his face and there was murder in it. Sea-Wyf was the only one who did not move.

"You know what it means?" Number Four asked in a harsh whisper.

"What?"

"That I drank your blood."

There was a moment of silence, and then the girl said calmly, "Please go back to your place."

"If you come with me," he whispered.

"Go back to your place."

Number Four rose up, balancing on his one leg. His arms drooped over her, fingers extended.

"Come with me."

"Go back to your place," she repeated breathlessly.

"Come with me," he said again. And then he added something in a strange language. It was a sound like falling stones. His leg bent at the knee as he leaned towards her.

Swiftly as a rising trout the girl came up and thrust against his chest. He staggered back. Bulldog was on his feet. There was a violent movement. The raft tilted and there was a splash. The water blazed.

Number Four came to the surface and gripped the side of the raft. Bulldog snatched up a stick which he must have worked loose from one of the fagots. He struck at the hands which grasped the float. Number Four grunted and backed away. He trod water, the sea burning round him.

"Sea-Wyf," he called urgently.

She did not answer.

"Sea-Wyf, listen here. Don't you know what it means to drink a person's blood. It means faithfulness. I'll die before I hurt you. You're the one person that's been good to me."

The girl moved.

"Take no notice," Bulldog said in a low, savage whisper. "He wanted you. He meant to kill Biscuit and me. He'd have grown strong eating us."

"Sea-Wyf," Number Four called again.

They saw him pause and lap some sea water to ease his throat. "Sea-Wyf, I'll do what you said. I never broke a promise. No violence. They'll be O.K.—those poor men—on the raft. And afterwards—it'll be legal. Legal only."

"Let him on board," Sea-Wyf pleaded.

Bulldog thrust her aside. He waved his stick at the man in the water.

"Get away, you swine!" he screamed. "You said you can't drown. Then swim!"

Number Four came slowly towards the raft, only his head showing. Bulldog crouched, waiting with the stick in his hand.

Number Four raised his right arm. The machete was in his hand and it seemed to drip with fire.

"Let me on board," he said.

"Get off. Swim to **Africa** where your slave ancestors came from," Bulldog shouted.

Number Four trod water, a collar of fire illuminating his face. Then his head sank slowly below the surface.

"You *must* let him on board. He'll drown. He is harmless as a child. It's just bravado. Please let him on board," Sea-Wyf was weeping.

Bulldog ignored her. He was waiting for Number Four to come up.

"Give me the water," Sea-Wyf said to Biscuit, suddenly determined. "Now hold him. Take that stick—"

She stopped short. They had all felt a strange vibration under the raft. Biscuit stooped to touch one of the lashings and it came up free in his hand. They felt another and another being cut.

Then Number Four surfaced, out of reach. He regained his breath. "You let me on board?" he asked.

"No! Swim off." Bulldog shouted.

Number Four dived again.

Again through their bare feet they felt the vibration of lashings being cut.

"If you won't let him on board from pity, do it for your life," Sea-Wyf cried. "He will drown us all."

"Not he. He can't cut the chain."

There was something wrong about that statement, Biscuit thought. But at the moment his troubled brain did not know what it was.

Number Four dived three times. On the fourth occasion he came up on a different side, close to the edge of the raft. He got his left arm on board. Bulldog leaped towards him. The machete flashed. Bulldog jumped aside and struck. Number Four vanished. The machete remained, quivering and buried deep in the woodwork. Bulldog wrenched it out.

Number Four came to the surface ten yards away. There was a savage majesty in his expression, lit by the shimmering fire.

"I curse you," he said. Then he lapsed into what sounded like the strange language he had used only a few minutes earlier on the raft.

None of them answered him. Although he was now harmless they all felt afraid.

Number Four began to swim away, leaving a line of fire behind him.

He stopped and called, "Sea-Wyf."

She was on her knees, sobbing. Her lips moved but no sound came out. She struggled up and would have thrown herself into the water if the others had not held her.

Number Four swam on. Even when they lost sight of his head they could see his burning wake and again and again they heard him call out, "Sea-Wyf," each time more despairingly.

They could not say when they last heard the call for it remained ringing in their ears, and until morning, when the phosphorescence faded, every disturbance of the water seemed to be made by Number Four.

It was not so bad while it was daylight, even though the raft was disintegrating under them as the wind gradually rose.

Biscuit realized what had been wrong with the statement that Number Four could not cut the chain. He had severed the weakest link, the place where the two ends had been bound together with rope. No important part of the raft had yet floated away. But the mast logs had begun to open and close like scissors. It was very clear what would happen when there was a storm.

Perhaps they should have dived and tried to mend things.

But none of them would go into the water. Besides, what could they achieve with a few short lengths of homemade rope?

In spite of these real dangers it was at sunset, at the time of issuing the water, that they were most disturbed. Biscuit bailed it out of the turtle shell which Sea-Wyf held. One, two three .... He did not measure a fourth, but he remembered the time, after the big storm on the float, when he had unconsciously broken off an extra ration of hardtack. Then in his exhausted mind there had been the impression that an extra person had helped them through the storm. Now the extra ration would have been for Number Four. None of them had liked him—except perhaps Sea-

Wyf with her infinite capacity for love. They had hated him, but he had been with them through everything. They had feared him. They feared him still.

None of them spoke, but their eyes wandered over the darkening sea. Thank God the phosphorescence had faded. But the growing darkness was bad enough.

The individual pieces of the raft were moving so much that there could be no possibility of sleep, exhausted though they were. They sat silent with their thoughts.

About the middle of the night, the wind still rising, they felt a sort of movement underneath them. There was a scraping sound. They listened, tense and still. Suddenly something broke surface close beside the raft. Bulldog leaped towards it grabbing up the machete.

It was the float. He caught hold of it.

When they had recovered a little Bulldog said, "I'd imagined this was the first thing he slashed to bits."

"He must have intended to save something until—" Sea-Wyf began.

"Until what?"

"Until I failed to answer him."

"Do not blame yourself," Biscuit said. "Let us get aboard."

They were in no state for a midnight transshipment, but they had nothing to carry except the turtle shell of water. So they got quickly away from the raft. It was a panic flight.

They scudded off before the wind. Time, which had

been vague since the sinking of the *San Felix*, ceased to have any meaning at all. It was a nightmare without question. The island and the raft were dreams within a dream. They had always been on the float and would be until they died.

All the pains and privations they had known returned to them in the most painful form—thirst, hunger, sores which turned to ulcers, and the fear of madness—the fear of madness most of all.

Bulldog was the worst. He had agonizing headaches. Often he was delirious. His lips, white and sticky, moved continually, though seldom could a word be distinguished. "Murder on the high seas" was the only phrase which the others remembered.

He had lucid moments during which, frantically licking his lips and trying to swallow, he told them that if they ever got anywhere they must make no mention of a fourth person having been with them, that they must part at once and hold no communication all their lives. "Biscuit—Sea-Wyf—Bulldog. Break-up-like-the-raft. Finish. Swear it."

They promised. They could not imagine any other life —only the sun roasting down and the eeriness of night when creatures splashed up phosphorescent waves and the wind seemed to be a voice which called a name . . . They agreed to everything which Bulldog demanded. If they demurred he would fall into a sudden, violent rage, trying to strike them as he had struck Number Four. Then it was only his weakness which prevented him from doing damage.

Biscuit and Sea-Wyf scarcely spoke at all. They sat

close together. Yet, somehow, she was farther away than ever. Sometimes it seemed to Biscuit that Number Four was there between them.

They felt perpetually exhausted and slept a great deal, fitfully. Once Biscuit was roused by the girl touching his arm.

"Good-by," she said.

Biscuit managed to turn himself and look at her. He thought she meant that she was going to die. But her face, the face of an old woman, was radiant.

"Good-by, Biscuit dear," she said, and although her eyes were shining they ran with tears. He wondered where they came from, those tears. So much water. . . .

It was sometime before he made out the smoke on the horizon. On several occasions during their long drift they had seen ships which had gone by. But this one was going to rescue them. They knew it. They roused Bulldog.

"Break up—like the raft—finish," he murmured.

The ship came closer. Biscuit took Sea-Wyf's hand and felt the surge of emotion which came from it. His eyes were bad and he had lost sight of the ship now because it was in line with the blazing sun.

Across the water came the ring of an engine room bell and the sound of voices, human voices.

Sea-Wyf drew her hand away. She began to smooth her hair and to gather together the tattered rags on her desiccated body.

CHAPTER TWENTY-FIVE

It was evening when Bulldog and Biscuit completed the first account of their experience. That account—dictated for a particular reason—was less full than the version I have given here, for I have added details which I learned afterwards and have tried without partiality to convey the characters as they appeared to me in the telling.

When the men stopped speaking I put down my pencil and went stiffly to the window—and it was a shock to look through rain-wet glass at the cold glitter of a calm northern sunset, for my mind was still in the Indian Ocean.

The others joined me.

A lighthouse began winking in the distance. Biscuit asked what it was. Bulldog said it marked a point on the Outer Hebrides.

The sea was smooth as a silver plate, its surface only broken by a ripple here and there, but below the castle it sighed as it caressed the seaweed rocks.

"What's that—at the mouth of the bay?" Bulldog asked. "Your eyes must be better than mine."

"A bird," I said. "A cormorant or a duck."

"It's making too much wash for a bird," Biscuit said. "Probably a seal—coming in to sleep on the rocks."

In silence we watched the leisurely departure of the day. Some hooded crows flapped slowly by, making for the woods behind the castle.

Bulldog went to the table and poured out a drink for me. We stood in the bay window, glasses in our hands.

"What a hell of an experience," I said. "To have to decide that one must kill a man. . . . But it was his life or yours."

There was another silence, and then Bulldog said, "We did not kill him."

"You mean—?"

"Number Four is alive. He reached land."

"Were there any ships about?" I asked after a pause.

"We saw no sign of ships for a week after that."

"How far were you from land?"

"A thousand miles."

I had been staring at Bulldog. He knew what my expression meant.

"I'm not mad," he said. "By God, no. I'm sane as can be."

"But how can Number Four be alive?" I asked.

"How should I know? Picked up somehow, I suppose." Bulldog answered with sudden impatience. "What matters is that he *is* alive. That's why we have to prepare a statement at once."

"Can you explain a little?" I said. "How do you know he is alive?"

"Because I have received a letter from him."

"A letter! Can I see it?"

SEA∤WYF

From his pocketbook Bulldog took a sheet of paper covered with pencil writing. It read as follows:

Bulldog:
    You think you have got rid of me but I follow you very very soon. You tried before to drown me. No good. I will have justice. I follow you to your own country and when you rise in the high place to give judgement I will cry out, "That is the man, who should be condemned. He tried to murder me." So I will drag you down. I can show proof. Right from the *San Felix*. I can prove everything.
    Biscuit will suffer also for his bad words and deeds. Only Sea-Wyf will I spare because she is for me and has told me beautiful things.
    I sign myself with the name you gave me.

                                            Number Four.

"It was posted in Mombasa on the eighteenth of last month," Bulldog said, taking the letter back. "So even if he traveled by tramp steamer he might arrive in this country at any moment."

"How did he know your address?" I asked.

"He once remarked that he knew everything about me," Bulldog said. "That is not true, of course. But as purser he knew my name and address—any fool could remember 'The Temple.' It was delivered to my chambers and was opened and forwarded by my clerk with other correspondence. He is a discreet fellow and only mentioned where and when this one had been franked and that he'd had to pay double postage. He can be trusted to keep his mouth shut. But I decided that it was my duty to warn Biscuit and Sea-Wyf that Number Four was alive and threatening us. In the strongest terms I requested their presence here for consultation and action. Biscuit responded at once, but —of course I do not know if Sea-Wyf received my letter. I still hope that she may come, however. We need her signature."

As he spoke the last sentence he turned away from me and looked again out of the window.

"Number Four is remarkably vague about the difference between an advocate and a judge," he said to the sunset. "Just like the damned fool. Thought himself so well informed . . . . Mentally, and educationally, he was about fourteen years old . . . . I wonder what was in his mind about the *San Felix*. There were no other survivors. I've made inquiries . . . . Of course there may be a passenger list in Singapore . . . . But he can't possibly have any case so long as we all say the same thing."

Bulldog went suddenly to the table and refilled his glass. He rejoined us in the bay window.

"Well, Scribe. You've got the story," he said almost jovially. "As I've told you, you can have all the facilities of my chambers for getting it typed, or you can use the machine here—just as you wish. But in any case"—he glanced at his watch——"Callum cannot have returned yet from Portree. No hope of dinner for an hour or more. Would you like to read back your notes to us, just to—to save any avoidable corrections later on?"

"Certainly," I said. The thought of getting back to work

was reassuring. "But could I just glance through them first? I took them down in a great hurry."

"Naturally," Bulldog answered. "Where would you like to sit?"

"Over there would do. May I turn on the light?"

Bulldog went to the door and flicked down the switch. Nothing happened.

"Damn and blast!" he shouted in a violent, embarrassing burst of anger. "The confounded idiots have cut us off again."

"You have got candles," Biscuit said, looking at him curiously.

Bulldog controlled himself. "Yes—yes I'm all too used to this." He went to a side table and lit some candles. I picked up a couple and took them to the second bay window, at the far end of the room. I placed one on each arm of the big leather chair and settled down with my notes on my knees.

I had intended to go right through the story, but what I found myself looking up was the conversation during which Number Four had said that he would never drown —that and the final scene when he had swum away, calling out Sea-Wyf's name.

The two men were talking only occasionally, and in low tones. I heard Bulldog ask Biscuit if he could still see the seal, and Biscuit answer that he could not, that it must have come ashore. A cork was drawn. Biscuit refused another drink, but I heard the hiss of soda as one glass was filled.

After that there was no sound for ten minutes or more.

Then there was a knock on the door.

It was an innocent enough sound but I started violently. I saw that the other two men had swung round to face the door.

The knock was repeated.

"Come in whoever you are," Bulldog shouted.

The door opened. Against the almost dark background of the anteroom stood a black figure with a glimmer of white about the face. Biscuit and Bulldog started forward with candles in their hands. They stopped two or three yards short of the figure, and I saw that it was a nun.

The two men stood staring.

"Sea-Wyf!" Biscuit said.

He took another rapid step towards her, then halted. His features were illuminated by his own candle, and I saw an amalgam of strong feelings on his face.

But Sea-Wyf was as undramatic and natural as could be. I had pictured her like that from what I had been told, but she was better than I had imagined. She stood with her hands folded, a graceful, peaceful figure in her long gown. As she answered Biscuit's questions I watched her face. It was extraordinarily mobile and sensitive. I noticed that more than the features. She smiled as she described her journey from London with another nun as companion, and Callum's shocked amazement when they approached the car. He had muttered strange words when she told him that his employer knew her as Sea-Wyf.

Callum's employer at that moment was slumped in a chair reviving his nerves with whisky, but Sea-Wyf was entirely unperturbed.

On the *San Felix*, she said, she had been returning with other nuns from their medical mission, and all except herself had been lost. In the float, on the island and the raft, she had concealed that she was a nun because, however well she behaved, it would have been a grave embarrassment for her order if it were known that one of its sisters had spent fourteen weeks with three men. That was why she had been so disturbed when she had recognized the words "holy woman" in Number Four's outburst to the submarine Commander. He had been saying, she believed, that she was an exceedingly saintly person (which, alas, she was not) and that the Japanese would be cursed forever if they did not make some offering. That was the hold which Number Four had had over her, his knowledge that she was a nun. But he had faithfully obeyed the command which she had given to him when they were swimming together. She had seen it as her duty to try to maintain peace between them to the end. Only by her final loss of faith and courage had she failed. She had suffered bitterly for that.

Biscuit asked how, being a nun, she had seen his announcements in the *Daily Telegraph*. She said that she worked as a nurse in a hospital and had overheard the patients talking about them.

The appeals had violently disturbed her in her quiet life, so much so that she had taken it upon herself to answer them and even to go to the market where she had seen Biscuit and Bulldog.

"But fortunately nobody notices the face of a nun," she said.

Most disturbing of all had been Bulldog's letter. She had felt that she must take it to the Mother Superior and her confessor, telling everything. And they, good and generous, had not only forgiven her but allowed her to travel north, with Soeur Mary as companion, to help wartime companions who seemed to be in grave distress.

Sea-Wyf had left Soeur Mary downstairs with Callum and his wife, and since she was of a nervous temperament she did not want to leave her long.

Bulldog scrambled to his feet.

"This is all very well," he said—and I knew by his voice that he was drunk at last. "But I called you two here to prepare a story that would stop Number Four making trouble —not that he could really do anything. We've dictated the story already. We shall need your signature, however."

"What makes you frightened?" Sea-Wyf asked.

"Frightened? I'm not frightened."

"You are frightened. Why?"

He stood staring at her, swaying a little.

"That letter of his," he said.

"What letter?"

"I've had a threatening letter from Number Four. That's why I wrote to you."

"May I see the letter, please?"

He took it from his pocketbook and handed it to her.

She studied it long and carefully while the two men beside her remained with their eyes intently on her face. She seemed deeply puzzled. She read it and reread it. She repeated one or two of the phrases aloud, though to herself. "You tried before to drown me . . . Only Sea-Wyf will I spare because she is for me and has told me beautiful things."

She looked up for a moment, with a flicker of understanding in her eyes and then began to study the letter again with a fresh intentness, the envelope and the paper. All the time the puzzled look was going from her face. It was replaced by one of sorrow.

"Poor Number Four," she said at last. "How hurt he was. But this shows he really did mean it when he said that he would only use legal means—"

"Legal!" Bulldog snorted. "He means to make trouble."

"He will not make trouble."

"You were always saying that, and he made all the trouble he could. If it were not for me who had the courage of my convictions we would all be dead."

"Number Four is dead," Sea-Wyf answered.

"Are you still trying to get the better of me. Do you think I am a fool?" Bulldog shouted.

Sea-Wyf made the very slightest movement with her shoulders.

"Could he swim to Africa through an ocean full of sharks?" she asked.

"But that letter . . . . It was posted less than a month ago."

"I do not think you are right. I believe it was posted when we were on the island."

"What do you mean?"

Instead of answering she turned to Biscuit and asked, "That iron box on the island—could it have been meant for letters?"

"Why, yes," he said. "Yes, I suppose it was."

"Then that is where he posted it," she said.

Biscuit looked at her, his face blank.

"But how could he have written it?"

"I could not imagine at first. But you remember when we found him with the knife he had a pencil stub—so proud that he could sharpen it. And about that time—I forget exactly when— I found that the flyleaf had been torn out of the Japanese book—"

"An envelope was in the book," Biscuit said thoughtfully, "With that message—"

"Which you translated, 'With love from Aunt Fanny'. Poor Number Four was very offended by the way he was treated on the island, when he could not get about. He told me that. And he had seen Bulldog try to hoist the sail when he swam back so bravely for the paddle. Of course I do not know when he wrote the letter, but—"

"It fits in," Biscuit said slowly. "Some ship has been round collecting turtles and copra and letters. That's the way the mail works in those lonely, timeless islands."

She nodded.

"Yes, it must have happened like that."

Bulldog had listened closely.

"If all that is true, Number Four could be dead after all," he said.

Sea-Wyf turned to him.

"Of course he is dead, poor man. But I trust his soul is in Heaven. I spoke to him much about the true God while we were on the island—those were the beautiful things he mentioned in the letter—and he said that he believed."

Bulldog gave a great shout.

"Ten to one it was collected by a black fellow who couldn't read. So there's nothing to worry about. Come on, let's celebrate!"

"Number Four is dead and everything is all right," Sea-Wyf said. Her hands were still clasped in front of her but she seemed to hold a scourge of cords. "We killed him, we three— I, since I lost my faith in him and was afraid because once on the island he had frightened me very much; Biscuit because he did nothing; you because you feared him most of all and planned his murder. You—God have mercy on you—also bore false witness. You drank the water—I saw you do it. You offered your ration to Biscuit and me, silently accusing him. Number Four was the one entirely honest person on the raft, and we must celebrate because he is dead, because I have convinced you that we killed him. Do you still doubt that I am right? What have I done penance for during these twelve years?"

She had spoken all this very quietly, not at all bitterly,

and the effect was stronger as a result. She stood waiting for a response. There was none.

"In his letter Number Four called for justice," she went on. "Poor, nameless, raceless man, what could he achieve if he were alive? But, as I stand here, I believe that he will find justice in the Courts of Heaven!"

That small, black-clothed figure with the quiet voice was the most powerful and moving thing that I have ever seen.

"She is right," Biscuit exclaimed excitedly. "Absolutely right. If she has done penance, what about you and me, Bulldog? Let us scrap that biased nonsense and tell the whole truth to the whole world. Let's get it off our chests at last!"

Bulldog looked at him with small and cunning eyes.

"You two always took sides against me," he said. "But I am not going to throw away all that I have built in a lifetime of hard work. You will sign what I tell you and keep your mouths shut. Twice you prevented me from neutralizing Number Four. But not now."

"It is not the dead man you need fear," Sea-Wyf said.

"Dead! That was a neat story you cooked up between you. It almost convinced me at first. You want to give Number Four the time he needs. But do you think I can't see through it? Do you think I'm mad?"

"Yes," Biscuit said. "I saw it coming on the raft."

Bulldog suddenly laughed. It was a startling sound.

"That's where you are wrong," he said, wagging a finger.

"I have seen both of you going mad for a long time—you trying to drown yourself and you muttering to yourself half the day. And the way both of you behaved when Number Four swam off. But I am absolutely sane. I realized why you were in such a hurry for us to get into the float—so that he could climb back onto the raft. Well, he is not coming here. I've got the courage of my convictions."

Bulldog strode to the window and stared out into the night. He pressed his two hands against the sides of his head.

Sea-Wyf whispered something to Biscuit.

Bulldog swung round.

"Stop plotting together! And don't argue with me. Do as I say or I'll—neither of you leaves this room until you sign what I tell you."

He went to the table and began to pour himself a drink.

But in the act of doing this he froze. We all started and then became quite still. From far below someone had called out "Sea-Wyf." The voice was blurred and indistinct with distance but there was no doubt about the name.

For a full minute we all remained listening intently . . . But there was only the soft sad whisper of the waves.

Then we heard another sound—a slow and heavy step mounting the stone stair. It came up to us through the open window, loudest when the step was on the outer side of the spiral, then fading, then loud again.

Bulldog was facing the door with the bottle still in his hand, and in that moment I felt I saw him standing on the raft, stick in hand, waiting for Number Four to surface.

The slow steps continued to spiral upwards until they reached the carpeted anteroom.

Then there was a moment of complete silence.

"Here he comes, but he shall not—"

The bottle smashed down upon the table edge and Bulldog crouched grasping the bottom half with the jagged daggers of glass projecting from it.

The door swung open. In the dark threshold where we had seen Sea-Wyf appear there was outlined the figure of a big man.

Bulldog rushed forward. Callum—for it was Callum—reacted with surprising speed and efficiency. He dropped the tray he was carrying, parried the blow and caught the wrist. But he could do little more until Biscuit and I joined him. At last, with sheets from the nearest bedroom, we had Bulldog trussed up like a mummy.

"It's a tarnation shame," Callum muttered. "The Nathams are the finest family in the world, but they all end the same way."

On his knees beside his master he surveyed us angrily.

"Why did ye no call me before? Surely ye saw it coming."

We did not answer.

"I called because the other papist lass is wanting ye—but ye would not hear ... It's just by that chance I came when I did. But if ye had called me in time I could have handled him."

He bent over the prostrate figure, then suddenly raised his arms and in a harsh and trembling voice demanded,

"What have ye done to him, ye daft, crazy people? Who are ye? What was it all about?"

Shortly after this the electric lights came on. We stood blinking at each other.